The Godmother

The Godmother

Tom Milton

NEPPERHAN PRESS, LLC
YONKERS, NY

Published by Nepperhan Press, LLC
P.O. Box 1448, Yonkers, NY 10702
nepperhan@optonline.net
nepperhan.com

PUBLISHER'S NOTE
This is a work of fiction. Names, characters, places, and incidents
are the product of the author's imagination or are used fictitiously,
and any resemblance to actual persons, living or dead, events, or
locales is entirely coincidental.

Printed in the United States of America

Library of Congress Control Number: 2018902498

ISBN 978-1-7320634-0-2

Cover art was licensed from Publitek, Inc.

For Marie

The beginning of love is to let those we love be perfectly themselves, and not to twist them to fit our own image. Otherwise we love only the reflection of ourselves we find in them.

Thomas Merton

Yonkers, 2014

ONE

WHEN HER GODDAUGHTER hadn't come home by six thirty Gina began to worry. The bodega where Marisol worked until six was only a five-minute walk from their house, and there wasn't any place where she would stop along the way.

At that point Gina texted the girl, asking: "Where are you?"

Texting was usually an effective way of contacting Marisol, so when there wasn't a response within ten minutes Gina began to worry more. If the girl had friends then there would be plausible explanations for her not coming directly home or not responding to a text message, but Marisol had no friends, at least no real friends from the neighborhood or from school—she only had "friends" she had met online, where she might have revealed too much about herself despite warnings about the predators who prowled the internet. So there were no friends for Gina to call and ask if Marisol was with them.

She would have liked to share the problem with her husband, Colman, who at this hour would usually be winding things down in an office that had replaced their garage, but he was at the courthouse helping a boy from the neighborhood who had gotten into trouble, so she had to deal with the problem herself.

Standing by the kitchen table, she called the bodega. The phone rang three times before the owner's wife answered, saying: "*Hola?*"

"*Hola, Belkis.* It's Gina. Is Marisol there?"

"No, she is not here." There was a pause. "She did not come to work today."

"Oh, I'm sorry. Did you see her?"

"No. I did not see her."

"Well, if you see her, could you ask her to call me?"

"Okay. I hope she is all right."

"*Gracias,*" Gina said, believing that Belkis cared about the girl.

Not knowing what else to do, Gina went upstairs to Marisol's room, where she encountered the domain of a teenager with bad hygiene habits. The girl had brought these habits with her from the home of her adoptive parents, and over the past four years Gina had tried to change them, but judging from the condition of the room, which smelled like an animal cage, she hadn't had much success.

Being orderly, even to the point where Colman teased her about being obsessive compulsive, Gina was dismayed by the chaos of the room. She had tried repeatedly to get Marisol to put her things in order, and every time she saw this mess of clothes and papers and plastic bags, it made her feel like a failure. But she didn't have time for her feelings, she had to look for clues that would help them find Marisol.

On the bed was the tangled zebra-print comforter that Marisol wrapped around herself like a cocoon. Usually a computer was on the bed, with the charger plugged into it, but it wasn't there, and it wasn't anywhere in the room. Marisol never took it to school because she had her smartphone to stay connected, and the only event scheduled for that day was rehearsal for graduation, which would be held on Friday at the campus of Mt. Saint Vincent. With classes over, Marisol didn't have to wear her uniform today, so she wouldn't have changed her clothes after school.

On a hunch Gina went to the bureau and opened the top drawer. Since she had done the laundry only yesterday, the drawer should have been full of underwear, but it was half empty, so the girl had taken a supply of underwear.

It was possible that she had gone to Sudbury to visit Ugo and Eileen, her adoptive parents, but it wasn't likely because she hadn't seen them in four years, and Gina couldn't think of anywhere else the girl might have gone.

Beginning to worry even more, she texted Colman, saying: "Please call me. It's urgent."

Within a few minutes her phone rang, and it was Colman.

"I don't know where Marisol is," she told him. "She didn't go to work after school. She came home, and she left with her computer. She took a supply of underwear, so she must have been planning to go somewhere."

"But where could she have gone? She has no friends."

"She has friends she met online."

"You think she went to see one of them?"

"I hope she didn't, but I don't know what else to think."

"I'll be right home. Don't worry. We'll find her."

Gina was reassured, having confidence in her husband who in his daily work was always solving problems, and while she waited for him to come home she searched her recent memory for clues about where Marisol might have gone.

During the past few months there hadn't been any notable changes in Marisol's behavior. She still resisted getting up in the morning to go to school. She still clung to the hope that if she was late enough then Colman would drive her to school, as he had at the beginning, but they were firm in trying to get her to assume some responsibility for her life, so they had given her no choice but to take the bus, and after being reported late a few times she managed to walk to Getty Square and catch the Bee-Line, number 6, which carried her up North Broadway to Shonnard, where she got off and walked to Sacred Heart High School.

She came home from school around three, taking the bus, and after changing out of her uniform she went to work at the bodega, over on Elm Street. She got the job there because Colman had done some pro bono legal work for Pascual, the owner, and of course because Marisol was fluent in Spanish. According to Belkis, the girl was fine with customers, always polite and respectful, though not very friendly except with the little kids who came into the store to buy candy. She was off at six and home within about five minutes. She came into the kitchen, knowing that Gina would be there making dinner, and said hello and then went up to her room and closed the door and lost herself in her computer, lying on her belly on the bed. She came downstairs for dinner, and though she couldn't wait to get back to her computer, Gina made her remain at the table until she and Colman were done eating. Marisol rarely initiated a conversation, but Colman got her to talk with them by speaking Spanish, and in her native language she became a different person, revealing a personality that didn't come out when she spoke English.

By now after living in this neighborhood with Colman for more than nine years, Gina was competent in Spanish. It had been an easy transition from Italian, which had been her first language growing up, and Colman joked that when she spoke Spanish she sounded like she was from Argentina, where they spoke with an Italian accent. So at home they often spoke Spanish with Marisol, figuring that she spent all day at school speaking English.

When she was excused from the dinner table Marisol went upstairs to her room and closed her door and returned to her computer. She spent the rest of the evening online, and when Gina knocked on her door and opened it to ask if she had done her homework, the girl always had the same answer: "Yeah. I did it before dinner."

Marisol could have done well at school, as indicated by tests for academic potential, and though she had a Latino accent she was fluent in English and even knew words of current slang that Gina didn't know, so there evidently wasn't a language problem. In fact, her best grades were in her English courses. But her grade-point average was stuck around C, as if that was the level she aimed for, and since she was graduating the next day there was no time left for improvement. While most of her classmates were headed for college, Marisol only reluctantly applied to St. Catherine, which accepted her because they were willing to give a chance to students who underperformed in high school.

Thinking about it, Gina wondered if the girl was worried about college. Though she had consciously tried not to put too much pressure on Marisol to go to college, maybe she had unconsciously projected her own thwarted dream of going to college. Maybe like mothers who projected their thwarted dreams of being singers, or

4

dancers, or actresses she had put intolerable pressure on Marisol to go to college.

But she wasn't the girl's mother, she was her godmother. And there was a difference, at least in theory. You had responsibilities, but you didn't have prerogatives. You could love your godchildren without hope that your life would be enhanced by their successes and without fear that it would be ruined by their failures.

So she worried now about the girl, not about herself.

She was still in Marisol's room, pacing around in a turmoil, when she heard Colman at the front door. She called to him, letting him know where she was, and she was calmed by the sound of him resolutely climbing the stairs.

"Did you hear from her?" he asked, entering the room.

"No. I've sent three text messages to her, and she hasn't responded."

He advanced toward her and put a reassuring hand on her shoulder. He was tall and lean, in very good shape for a man who had just turned sixty-two. "Well, maybe she didn't get your messages. Maybe the battery in her phone is dead."

"Yeah, maybe," she said hopefully. The girl was always letting the battery in her phone run down and then ransacking her room for the charger. Gina had lost count of the times they had to buy another charger.

"Did you find any more clues?" he asked, looking around the room methodically.

"No. There's only the missing underwear."

He frowned in concentration. "Do you think she could have gone to Sudbury?"

"She could have, but it's not likely. And if she was planning to go there, why wouldn't she have told us?"

"She knew we wouldn't be happy about it."

"We never stopped her from going there. We even suggested that she go and spend a weekend there, but she never wanted to. And they never invited her."

"But they could have invited her," Colman persisted.

"They said they were done with her," Gina reminded him.

"Since she's graduating from high school, they could have changed their minds."

"I doubt it. And even if they had, with graduation tomorrow they wouldn't have invited her to go there today. They would have invited her to go there on Saturday."

"They could have invited her to spend the night, intending to bring her back tomorrow for graduation."

Still resisting the possibility, Gina said: "If they invited her, they would have told us."

"Maybe she was supposed to tell us."

This scenario was plausible because the girl had never been an effective conduit of information between the two households, as much as Eileen had tried to use her for that purpose before giving up on her. "So how would she have gotten to Sudbury?"

"They could have picked her up."

"You mean here?"

"Yeah, or at school."

"If they picked her up at school, then they brought her here. She got her computer and packed some underwear. And what if I'd come home and found them here?"

"As far as they knew, they wouldn't have been doing anything behind your back. They would have assumed that Marisol told you she was going to spend the night with them."

Gina considered. "I guess it's possible, but it's not likely."

"I know it's not likely," Colman agreed, "but before we start looking elsewhere, we need to rule out the possibility."

"All right," Gina said, accepting the logical process he used in his professional life. "I'll call Eileen, though I don't like getting her involved."

"If Marisol is missing, we have to get Eileen involved. We may need information from her."

"What kind of information?"

"Whatever she knows about Marisol that we don't know, beginning with her adoption."

Gina understood because their minds were evidently running in the same direction. "Okay. Let's go downstairs. I need to get out of this room."

Colman put his arm around her and guided her out into the hall and followed her down the stairs. They went to the kitchen, where they sat down at the table on which there was a stack of magazines and a scatter of notes reminding them to do things. They had breakfast individually at this table, and they had dinner together at the table in the dining room, following the tradition of the two-family home in Throgs Neck where Gina had grown up, except that then there were seven people at the dinner table and now there were only three.

Before dialing the number, Gina tried to remember the last time she had talked with Eileen. She thought it was when they needed a copy of Marisol's birth certificate to renew her passport. Eileen hadn't been cooperative. And all the times before, Eileen hadn't been cooperative. It was if Eileen, after saying they were done with Marisol, still wanted to retain control over her, maybe still hoping she could make the girl fit the image of what she had wanted in adopting a child.

While waiting for someone to answer the phone Gina thought about how to delay getting Eileen involved in the situation, and she had an idea by the time one of the twins answered. They sounded alike as much as they looked alike, so Gina didn't even try to guess which one it was. She only said: "Hi, honey. It's Aunt Gina. How are you?"

"I'm fine, thanks," the voice said in a self-assured Connecticut accent. "How are you?"

"I'm fine. Could I speak with your mother?"

"Yes, just a minute please."

She looked across the table at Colman as she waited for Eileen to get on the line. With his closely trimmed gray hair she thought he looked like a retired general, and knowing what he did for people she could understand why he was universally respected in the neighborhood.

"Hello?" Eileen said guardedly.

"Hi," Gina said. "I hope I didn't interrupt your dinner."

"No. The kids have eaten."

From what she had observed in that house, Gina could imagine what the kids had eaten—frozen pizza warmed in a microwave oven, washed down with Mountain Dew. "I called to ask you a question. Marisol told us she was going to spend the night with you. Is that true?"

"No, it's not true," Eileen said without hesitation. "Why would she have told you that?"

"I don't know," Gina said tensely. "Maybe she's hoping for an invitation."

"Well, she's not going to get one. We have a full house now."

"Okay. I just wanted to know what was happening."

"You better watch out for her. She never tells the truth."

Gina felt like saying that from her experience Eileen was the one who never told the truth, beginning with her reasons for adopting Marisol and ending with her reasons for abandoning the girl. But she didn't say it. She ended the call and told Colman: "They didn't invite her."

"So we can rule out that possibility."

Boiling with anger, Gina said: "I really can't stand that woman."

"Her problem is, she's shanty Irish wannabe lace-curtain Irish." Being Irish, he could get away with saying this. "She only wanted children so that she could meet the parents of their friends. Since Marisol had no friends, she wasn't useful, and since she wasn't white, she didn't fit their image."

"Then why did they adopt a girl who wasn't white?"

"Maybe at the time they felt she was better than nothing."

"Well, let's not talk about them. Let's talk about how we're going to find our goddaughter."

It didn't take them long to decide that they should call a police detective whom Colman worked with frequently. His name was Ron, and about once a week he would drop by the house and go into Colman's office and have a coffee and share information about what was happening in the neighborhood. From people who had grown up there, Gina knew that a generation ago it had been a neighborhood of Poles and Italians, who except for a few aging survivors had dispersed to suburban areas of Westchester County to raise their families or to retire. When Gina told people who knew Yonkers that she lived on Nodine Hill, they usually reacted by shaking their heads in sympathy or amazement. It was a neighborhood that kept the police busy, though it wasn't the worst in Yonkers, and it wasn't as bad as some areas in Mount Vernon, at least in terms of the crime rate.

Gina lived there because it was where Colman lived when she met him, and Colman lived there not because he had grown up there—he had grown up in an Irish neighborhood of the Bronx—but because he had a mission, and he had bought the house at the time the neighborhood was changing, anticipating its need for legal services. He could have lived in another area and rented an office downtown, but that would have removed him from the people he served, and it would have placed an obstacle between him and them. So he lived among them, maintaining his office in his home where people who needed his services could walk to it.

Ron didn't walk there, he arrived in his unmarked black Crown Victoria, which he parked on the street as he always did. Of course the neighbors knew it was a cop car, and most of them welcomed its presence on the street because it made them feel the police were watching out for them. And since they trusted Colman, they trusted Ron by association.

"Hello," Ron called to them through the screen door.

"Come in," Colman called back to him.

They met the detective in the hallway. Ron was a solid man with a lined face and deep-set eyes. By now he could have retired from the force, but he loved his work and was good at it, so he kept doing it.

"Thank God you're on duty," Colman said.

"I'm always on duty," Ron said. He was followed by his partner, Emilio, a young Latino with closely shorn dark hair and hot dark eyes. "So what's happening?"

"As I told you on the phone, we don't know where our

goddaughter is. She didn't come home when she was supposed to, and she doesn't respond to text messages."

"That's not normal," Ron said, shaking his head. "Kids always respond to text messages. In fact, they respond even when they're driving cars."

"Yeah, last week," Emilio said, "a kid ran into a telephone pole on Nepperhan Avenue while responding to a text. He's lucky his car veered to the right, or he could have had a head-on."

"The battery in her phone could be dead," Colman said.

"Yeah, it could be," Ron said. "When was she supposed to come home?"

"She works at the bodega on Elm Street," Gina said, "and she's off at six. It usually takes her about five minutes to walk home."

"Is that the bodega owned by Pascual?"

"Yeah. She goes there after school."

"Did she go there today?"

"No. When she wasn't home by ten of seven I called the bodega, and Belkis told me she didn't come to work today."

Ron paused to think. "What time did you get home?"

"Around five thirty, as usual."

"Did you notice anything wrong?"

"No. I changed my clothes and went to the kitchen and started making dinner."

"You assumed that she was at work?"

"Yeah. I had no reason to assume otherwise."

Ron paused again. "Did she usually come home from school before she went to work?"

"Oh, yeah. She came home to get out of her uniform."

"I understand. My girls just couldn't wait to get out of their uniforms."

"I couldn't either," Gina admitted. But she didn't go so far as to say that along with her friends she had rolled up the top of her skirt to make it shorter.

"So you called the bodega," Ron continued. "Did you call her friends?"

"She has no friends."

Ron looked at her sadly. His daughters had finally made it to their late twenties and become less of a worry to him, but he knew what it was like having teenage girls. "Then let's try to find some clues. Does she have a computer?"

"Yeah, but she took it with her."

"Does she keep a diary?"

"I don't think so. At least I never saw one."

"Well, let's go and look at her room."

"It's a mess," Colman warned him.

"I know what to expect," Ron said. "My wife tried to get our kids to clean up their room, and she never succeeded. They have their own apartment now, and it's neat as a pin."

"You mean there's hope," Emilio said as if he had his own problems.

"There's always hope with kids."

Gina led the way upstairs and into Marisol's room, repressing the urge to apologize for the way it looked.

"I've seen worse," Ron said.

"So have I," Emilio said.

"Besides the computer, did she take anything else with her?"

"She took some underwear," Gina said, "so she must have been planning to stay with someone."

"If she has no friends, who would she stay with?"

"We have no idea," Colman said. "We ruled out the possibility that she went to Connecticut to spend the night with her adoptive parents, so we're left with the possibility that she went to stay with someone she met online."

Ron nodded. "When they're online, the kids reveal things about themselves, and there are people sifting through the information, looking for a way to meet them face to face."

"For what purpose?" Gina asked, though she could guess.

"To swindle money from them, or to lure them into a situation where they can be used for commercial purposes."

"You mean pornography?"

"Yeah, or prostitution."

"But it could be just another kid who has no friends."

"It could be. You never know who these people are until you meet them face to face. I mean, they all pretend to be something they aren't."

"I wonder what our goddaughter pretends to be," Gina mused, heartsick.

"Search the desk," Ron told his partner, "and see if you can find a diary. My girls both kept diaries."

"Did you ever read them?" Colman asked.

"I was tempted to, but I never did. There's such a thing as too much information."

"There's also such a thing as too little information," Emilio said, looking at the desk. "How old is your kid?"

"She's eighteen," Gina told him.

"Is she still in high school?"

"Yeah, but she graduates tomorrow."

"I don't see any homework here."

"She did her homework on her computer. She printed her papers in Colman's office."

"Do you have copies of her papers?"

"No," Colman said. "She kept her papers on a flash drive, so I don't have them on my computer."

"That's too bad," Ron said. "There might have been something in one of her papers that would give us a clue about where she went."

"I read all her papers," Gina said. "She always asked me to review them. She didn't want to make mistakes in English."

"Do you remember anything that would give us a clue?"

"No. The papers weren't about her. There were about the readings in her courses."

"From what you say," Emilio said, "her first language wasn't English."

"It wasn't. Her first language was Spanish."

"Where was she from?"

"Honduras."

"Really? Where in Honduras?"

"San Pedro Sula."

12

Emilio shook his head, frowning. "That's a bad place. It has the highest murder rate of any city in the world."

"Gina, refresh my memory," Ron said after giving his partner a look that warned him not to be so insensitive in his remarks. "As I recall, the girl was adopted by your brother and his wife when she was about six."

"She was almost seven."

"And four years ago they decided they didn't want her?"

"That's right. They always had trouble with her, and after they had their own children they had no further use for Marisol."

"How many children do they have?"

"They have twin girls and a boy."

"You mean after they had three white children, they didn't want a brown child," Emilio muttered, looking into a drawer of the desk.

"I'll pretend I didn't hear that," Ron told him.

"And I'll pretend I didn't say it."

"So she was abandoned by her birth mother, and then she was abandoned by her adoptive mother. The poor kid."

"She has a lot of problems," Gina said. "We gave her a safe haven, and we gave her love. But I don't know if she understands the meaning of love."

"She had no prior experience with love," Colman said.

"I thought we were making some progress, but now I wonder."

"The only thing I found in the desk," Emilio said, "was an empty Red Bull can."

"I thought we got her off that," Gina said.

"It could have been in the desk for a while," Colman said.

"Do we agree," Ron asked after a silence, "that the most likely scenario is that the girl went to stay with someone she met online?"

Gina and Colman exchanged a look, and then she said: "Yeah, we agree."

"The problem is, the person she met could be anywhere."

"So where are we going to look for her?" Emilio asked, turning his attention to the pile of clothes on the floor.

"We need to figure out what bait this person used to lure her."

"It had to be something she wanted," Colman said.

"She wanted a friend," Gina said.

"But she didn't do anything to make friends."

"She was afraid of being rejected. The kids in Sudbury treated her like shit."

"What about Facebook?" Ron asked.

"What about it?" Gina said.

"Does she have a Facebook page?"

"I guess she does. I never saw it, but all the kids have Facebook pages, so she must have one."

"If she does have one, I have a computer geek who can find it."

"Even if she used a different name on it?"

"If you give me information about her computer, he can find her Facebook page whatever name she used on it."

"Can he find out where she is?" Colman asked hopefully.

"I don't know," Ron said. "I'm not a geek."

"If she uses her computer," Emilio said, "he can probably find her. But if she doesn't use it, he can't find her. There has to be a signal to track."

For the first time ever Gina hoped the girl would spend all night on her computer.

"But whether or not she uses her computer," Colman said, "he can find her Facebook page?"

"Yeah, he can," Ron said. "And that should give us a list of her online friends."

"Well, I have all the information about her computer. I can't tell you how many times I've had to take her to the Apple store to have it fixed."

"Apple makes crappy products," Emilio said, kneeling on the floor to confront the mess. "Outside they appeal to the eye, but inside they're junk."

"You could say that about a lot of products," Ron said. "They look good, but they don't last."

While Colman went down to his office to get the information about the computer, Emilio patiently sifted the mess and Ron made notes on their conversation.

Gina stood there returning to the question of what bait the person had used to lure her goddaughter. A promise of friendship? A promise of love? The more she thought about it, the more she doubted that such promises would have been enough because Marisol had learned not to trust people who claimed to love her. It must have been something she yearned for at a deep level, presented in a package that had allayed the suspicions that flickered in her dark eyes even when she opened Christmas gifts.

"Hey," Emilio said. "I found something."

Gina stared at the little black object with a dangling cord that he held up as if it was a rodent. "It's the charger for her phone."

"Then maybe her phone is dead."

"Maybe. But that could be the charger she lost two weeks ago."

"So we don't know," Ron said, "if she's not responding to your messages because her phone is dead or because she decided not to respond."

Though it hurt Gina to believe that the girl had decided not to respond, it also gave her hope because if the battery wasn't dead at least she would be able to respond. And it didn't seem likely that she had gone to stay with someone without taking a charger for her phone as well as a charger for her computer.

"I have the information," Colman said, returning. "I have the model number, the serial number, and some other numbers."

"That's great," Ron said, taking the paper with the information. He studied it briefly, and then he said: "I also need a photo of the girl."

"A digital photo?" Gina asked.

"Yeah, that would be a lot better than having to scan an analog photo."

Gina always had photos in her phone, so she looked through them and found a photo of Marisol that she had taken a few weeks ago when they were having dinner at Caridad, a Dominican restaurant on South Broadway. By making a ridiculous face Gina had coaxed a rare smile out of the girl. "Where should I send this?"

"Send it to my phone," Ron said. He gave her the number.

She sent the photo to his number.

"Got it. Thanks. We'll circulate this photo tonight, and tomorrow morning we'll have our geek look for her Facebook page."

"Is there anything we can do in the meantime?"

"Yeah, you can hope she responds to your messages. And you can pray."

They followed the police downstairs and thanked them at the door, which they didn't close and lock until the car drove away.

Then Colman put his arms around her and said: "Don't worry. We'll find her."

"Why didn't she tell us where she was going?"

"Maybe she was afraid we'd stop her."

"We couldn't stop her," Gina said. "She's of legal age. She can go wherever she wants. So she must have had another reason for not telling us."

"Well, maybe she didn't want to hurt us."

"You mean by leaving us?"

"I mean by going wherever she went."

"But where could she go that would hurt us?" Gina asked, drawing her head back from his shoulder and appealing to his kind blue eyes.

"She could go to find her mother," Colman said, unveiling the answer that had formed in the shadows of her mind.

"You mean her birth mother."

"I don't mean Eileen."

"But her mother died in a car accident."

"That's what Eileen told us. And maybe it's true. But if you were Marisol, would you believe what Eileen told you?"

"No, I wouldn't," Gina said, remembering times when the girl had said she didn't believe her mother died in a car accident. "So maybe someone online lured her by saying he knew where her mother was."

"It's just a theory," Colman cautioned her.

"But it makes sense. I mean, nothing else makes sense."

"Her mother could be still alive. Eileen could have lied to us, or the lawyer who handled the adoption could have lied to her."

"Why would he have lied to her?"

"To expedite the deal. And ultimately to stop Marisol from trying to find her mother."

"So if we don't trust them," Gina said, "then we should be able to understand why Marisol doesn't trust them."

"And why she doesn't trust us," Colman added. "When she asked us what happened to her mother, we only repeated what Eileen told us."

"Well, we believed what Eileen told us, and we still don't have any reason not to believe it."

"But if Marisol doesn't believe it, that's what matters."

"Yeah, you're right," Gina said.

"I'll call Ron and tell him our theory. It'll help them focus their investigation. And if it's wrong, they'll be able to prove it."

"You mean by getting evidence that her mother did die in a car accident?"

"Yeah. Though it might not help us find Marisol."

Gina understood. If there was such evidence, it wouldn't stop the girl from trying to find her mother unless they could find her and present it to her. And to find her, they had to find the person who had lured her wherever she had gone.

TWO

AFTER HEARING THEIR theory Ron gave them assignments to help him with the investigation, so while Colman went into his office to look through the papers that Eileen had given them in a Talbots bag when she dumped Marisol on them, Gina went upstairs to look for Marisol's passport, which she kept in the top drawer of the bureau in their bedroom hidden under Colman's socks. And she found that Marisol's passport was missing.

She stood at the bureau remembering how they had renewed the passport so that they could take her to Punta Cana for her spring break. The original passport had been issued more than ten years earlier at the time of Marisol's adoption, and it had expired. The process of renewing the passport should have been simple, except that Ugo and Eileen had changed her name to Meredith as if somehow that would transform an unruly brown girl who played soccer with boys into a docile white girl who played field hockey with girls.

Marisol had never accepted the name change, and for almost every purpose including school and the bank she used her original given name, so the need to renew her passport was an opportunity to set things right. The process required several documents, including her birth certificate, which Eileen refused to hand over until Colman threatened to report her to social services. And even with all the documents, it took him months to reverse the name change and get a new passport for the girl.

Gina's next stop was in the small bedroom that she used as an office. She sat down at her computer, turned it on, and waited for it to start up. They had wireless service in the house from a router in Colman's office, which using the Spanish pronunciation they

18

called "wee-fee." Gina opened her browser and went to the site of their bank accounts. She was a joint tenant on the account in which Marisol deposited the money she earned from her job at the bodega, and though Gina had online access to it, she rarely looked at the account, respecting the girl's privacy. But now she could justify checking the account, and when she got into it she found that the girl had been withdrawing two hundred dollars in cash from the machine about twice a week over the past several weeks. Before, she had withdrawn money only about twice a month, and only in amounts of fifty dollars. Adding up the recent withdrawals, Gina arrived at a total of two thousand dollars—enough to buy a plane ticket to almost anywhere.

After signing off on the accounts Gina hurried downstairs to Colman's office, where she found him with papers spread across his desk as if in preparation for a trial.

"She took her passport," Gina told him, "and she withdrew two thousand dollars from her bank account."

"Two thousand dollars?"

"Yeah. She withdrew it over the past several weeks, two hundred dollars at a time."

"If she'd withdrawn it all at once, you would have noticed."

"I wouldn't have noticed, but the bank would have."

Colman shook his head. "They would have noticed only if she'd wanted to take all the money out of the account. They would have needed your signature for that."

"So she has enough money for a plane ticket."

"Well, you found out more than I did. I only found out the name and address of the lawyer who handled the adoption."

"That could be useful."

"It could be. I mean, if he cooperates."

Colman called the information service and got the lawyer's phone number. Since it was after nine there was no point in trying to reach him now, but Colman said he would try in the morning. Then he called Ron and reported that Marisol had taken her passport and withdrawn two thousand dollars from her bank account. Ron said his computer geek had left for the day but would return the next morning to look for the girl's Facebook page. He would call them as soon as he had any news.

There was nothing more they could do now but hope and pray, so Gina toasted two slices of filone and made an omelet, which they ate in the kitchen. From then until they went to bed around midnight she sent a text message to Marisol about every half hour. But there was no response. And whenever she tried calling on the phone she got the kind of busy signal you got when the number you were calling wasn't in service.

Lying awake in bed that night, Gina wondered how far back into the past she had to go in order to understand the present. To the time when Marisol came to live with them after Ugo and Eileen decided they were done with her? To the time when Marisol was adopted? To the time when Gina, her sister, and her brother were living with their parents in the two-family house in the Bronx? To the time when their grandparents came to America from a village south of Naples to pursue their dream of a better life?

Since Gina couldn't go back any further, she started with her grandparents, Matteo and Luisa Moretti, who left their native country in 1906 with nothing more than the skills they had learned from plying their trades, Matteo as a stone mason for a prominent builder and Luisa as a housekeeper for a noble family. Though they were in their early twenties, they already had valuable skills because they had been working since their mid-teens, and it didn't take them long to find jobs in New York. Within five years they bought a two-family house in Throgs Neck together with a cousin, who lived in the bottom half with his family, while they moved into the top half, planning to start their own family.

By the time Luisa had her first baby they no longer needed her income, so she became a full-time mother and housewife, and she not only ran the house, she ruled it. There was only one way of doing things, and that was her way. She was barely five feet tall, but she ordered big men around as if they were children. And she was quick to categorize people, applying the standards she had picked up from the noble family according to which almost everyone belonged to a lower class than she did. She had a whole vocabulary of words for denigrating people because of where they came from, where they lived, or what they did for a living. She rarely had a good word to say about anyone.

In contrast, Matteo was a man of few words. He talked only when he had something to say, and since Luisa hardly ever stopped talking he didn't get many opportunities to talk. He sat across the table from her pretending to listen while in his mind he might have been working on a project, figuring out how to fit two stones together. He puffed on his pipe and nodded his head in formal acknowledgment of what his wife said, but he never interrupted her, and he never corrected her, even when her statements were preposterous.

Luisa had five girls before she finally had a boy. They named him Gianni after Matteo's father who was still living in Italy, and since he was the only male in his generation they treated him like royalty. Luisa, who was extremely hard on the girls, let Gianni get away with anything. And though his older sisters might have envied the attention he got, they couldn't help spoiling him with their own attention.

When Gianni reached his teens, Matteo tried to apprentice him as a stone mason, but it soon became evident that Gianni was no good at working with his hands. Like his mother, he was good at talking. He was also good at entertaining people, and believing he had a lot of talent, his mother had him take singing lessons. After a concert he gave at the high school people were wondering if he could make it to Broadway. Matteo doubted that his son could earn a living as an entertainer, and he made a last, futile effort to train Gianni as a stone mason.

At that time most people didn't go to college, so when Gianni graduated from high school he was expected to go to work. He got a job in the men's department at Macy's, and it didn't take him long to establish himself as one of their top salespeople. He would have gone far at Macy's if the war hadn't interrupted his career, but at least he was able to use his talent in the army, not to entertain the troops but to serve as the driver and interpreter for a colonel in the Italian campaign. So he emerged from the war unscathed, with a lot of stories to enthrall people.

Instead of returning to his old job, he took a position as a salesman for a distributor of kitchen equipment, with a territory that included New York City. He earned good commissions, and since he still lived at home with his parents he had money to pay for fashionable clothes, restaurant meals, Broadway shows, and presents for girlfriends. His parents were beginning to wonder if he would ever get married when in 1954 he met a girl from the neighborhood who worked as a seamstress in the Garment District. Her name was Assunta, and her family had emigrated a year ago from postwar Italy, with their entry into the United States facilitated by an army officer whose life had been saved by her father. Attracted by her pristine beauty, Gianni fell in love with Assunta, but when he brought her home to meet the family he encountered fierce resistance from his mother, who didn't think Assunta was good enough for her son. To begin with, Assunta was from Sicily, which Luisa didn't consider part of Italy but an extension of Africa—the fact that Assunta had blond hair, blue eyes, and fair skin didn't seem to grant her membership in the white race. To make things worse, Assunta worked at a lowly job in an industry that was run by Jews. And on top of everything her family lived in the post-war project that was built in Throgs Neck for low-income families. So for two years Luisa stood in the way of her son's desire to marry Assunta until finally she succumbed to his endless onslaught of tearful claims that if he couldn't have Assunta he would die, and in 1956 they were married at St. Frances de Chantal.

By then his sisters were married and living in their own homes, so his parents moved to the bottom half of the two-family house and the newly married couple took over the top half. Gina was born in 1958, and Leonora was born in 1960. It took until 1965 to fulfill Gianni's dream of having a son and his parents' dream of having a grandson. They named him Ugo after one of Luisa's grandfathers, who had recently died.

Gianni was one of those men who believed that his duties to his wife and children didn't go much beyond providing money for them to live on. He worked late, and usually he had dinner with friends at a restaurant on Arthur Avenue or he played cards at the local Italian club. But he was always present at the family dinners on Thanksgiving, Christmas Eve, Palm Sunday, and Easter as well as at the family picnics on Memorial Day, Fourth of July, and Labor Day.

He was generous with his children, especially on Christmas and on their birthdays, but he hardly ever did things with them. It was his job to bring home the money, and it was Assunta's job to raise the children. He gave his wife an allowance to buy food and other essentials, while he kept the rest of his paycheck for discretionary spending. He didn't believe in saving for a rainy day, and luckily, at least for a while, their lives were filled with sunshine.

Prodded by Assunta, he sent his children to Catholic schools, beginning with St. Frances de Chantal School, which was in the neighborhood. Gina was in fifth grade at this school when her father was promoted to regional manager of the kitchen equipment distributor. As a manager he was paid a higher salary, which he needed to support his family and send his children to Catholic schools, but he wasn't as happy as he had been as a salesman, and he couldn't go any higher in the company because it was family owned. So he found other outlets for his energy, which included doing sessions at a recording studio and making his family listen to his tapes. His mother, whom his children called Nonna, told him he could be the next Sinatra, while his father, whom they called Nonno, only puffed his pipe in silence.

Finally, after he had made the family listen to yet another tape, his father said: *"Tu non sei felice nel tuo lavoro."*

"What makes you say I'm not happy in my work?"

"If you were happy, you wouldn't make these bad recordings."

"They're not bad, they're good."

"Who says they're good?"

"My sound engineer says they're good."

"Of course he does. You're paying him to make them."

23

"And people at the company say they're good."

"They have to. They work for you."

"Well, mama says they're good."

With a faint smile Nonno said. "If you shit on the floor, she'd say it was good."

"Okay, okay. So we have different tastes in music. And I'll admit that I was happier as a salesman than I am now."

"Then why don't you go back to sales?"

"I can't. I need the money I'm making now."

"I raised six children as a stone mason, and I was always happy in my work. You're raising three children, and you're not happy in your work. There's something wrong."

"The world has changed," Gianni said. "It's not like it was when you were raising children. It's tougher now."

"You think it's tougher now than it was during the Depression? If you do, then you don't have a very good memory."

"Well, things didn't cost as much then."

"People didn't make as much money then."

"Okay, okay. You made your point. I'll think about it."

Gianni may have thought about it, but it took him several years to do something about it. Gina was in high school when he started his own business. It was a retail store on East 53rd Street between Lexington Avenue and Third Avenue that sold kitchen equipment to households. At the time there were only a few other stores in the city that served this market, and now that even wealthy people were doing some cooking, they cared about what they had in their kitchens and they were attracted by European design.

The whole extended family went to the grand opening of the store, including Gianni's sisters and brothers-in-law and their children. There were platters of bruschetta and glasses of Prosecco passed around by men in white coats, and tapes of arias sung by Pavarotti playing in the background. The store was stocked with a wide variety of pots and pans and bowls and utensils, mostly imported from Italy and France, as well as kitchen towels, napkins, and table settings. The main attractions were a machine for making

24

home-made pasta that cost two hundred and ninety-five dollars and an espresso machine that cost even more.

At one point her father cornered Gina and asked: "*Cosa ne pensi di questo?*"

"What do I think of it?" Gina repeated, thrown off balance by the question. Her father had never given her any reason to expect that he would value her opinion on such a matter, though as far back as she could remember he had given her the feeling that he relied on her in ways that he couldn't rely on his other two children. "I think it could be a big success. I mean, if there are enough people who have the money to buy these things."

"There are enough people who have the money," her father assured her. "And they all want to have these things in their kitchens."

"Then it'll do well," Gina said, hoping it would.

Initially, the store lost money, and since Gianni had no reserves, he borrowed from relatives to keep the business going and support his family. More than once Assunta offered to go back to work as a seamstress in the Garment District, but Gianni wouldn't hear of it, and Nonna went berserk at the mere mention of the possibility that her daughter-in-law would disgrace the family by doing work that in her mind was only a step above cleaning houses.

"It's all right for Chinese and Puerto Ricans to do that kind of work," Nonna proclaimed, "but it's not all right for Italians."

"It's the only work I know how to do," Assunta said.

"Then stay at home and take care of your family. I never went back to work after I had my first baby."

"But we don't have enough money to live on, and we're going deeper into debt."

"The store will succeed," Nonna assured her. "My son has never failed at anything."

The store was still losing money when Gina graduated from high school. She was planning to go to college, though she knew her father opposed the idea, not only because the family needed the income she could earn from a full-time job but also because her father believed that girls didn't need a college education. When she broached the idea with him, he said: "You don't need college. You have enough education for a girl."

"I don't agree with you," she argued. "Girls need the same education as boys."

"You don't know what you're talking about," he told her. "Girls only need an education to be wives and mothers. It's a waste of money for them to go to college."

"If I go to college, I can get a better job."

"You can get a good enough job with a high school diploma. And we made a lot of sacrifices to send you to Preston."

Her mother intervened on her behalf, but as things turned out, the needs of the family prevented Gina from going to college, and a few weeks after her graduation she found a job in Manhattan as secretary for the man in charge of production at a large international printing company. She kept ten percent of her salary for herself and contributed the rest to the family. In fact, for a while her salary was the family's only source of income.

The store continued to struggle for the next two years, and Gianni continued to borrow from relatives to keep it going. Then one fine day Jacqueline Kennedy came into the store looking for a special pan that was made in France, and she not only found it, she told all her friends about the store. It wasn't long before "Gianni Moretti" was as well-known as any designer store on Madison Avenue, and Gianni became rich and famous.

Among his clients he couldn't admit that he lived in the Bronx, and meanwhile a lot of Puerto Ricans had moved into the neighborhood, so he decided that it was time to leave the Bronx, and he bought a mansion on Palmer Road in Yonkers that was rumored to have been built by a mafia don. It had two stone lions guarding the entrance.

His parents didn't want to leave their neighborhood, so they stayed in the bottom of the house and rented the top to a young couple. The rent, together with their social security, provided them with enough income to live comfortably, but Gianni gave them additional money, which they used mainly for improvements to the house. At one point he bought them first-class plane tickets to Naples and booked them in a luxurious hotel, so that they could revisit their home country, which they hadn't seen in seventy-two years. But they were in their mid-nineties, and though they were both in good health, they didn't have the energy for such a trip. And besides, they said, everyone they had known there long ago was probably dead.

For the next two years Gianni spent his money lavishly. He furnished the house as if it was a palazzo in Naples. He bought designer clothes for himself and his wife. He went on trips to Italy and France, booking the expenses as tax deductions because he was ostensibly looking for new products to offer. And he gave parties, culminating in a party at the Waldorf Astoria for two hundred guests, about half of whom were members of his extended family and the other half, suppliers and customers of his store. Of course he invited Jacqueline Kennedy, and though she didn't attend the party, a few of her friends did.

He insisted that his parents attend, and he hired a limousine to bring them to Manhattan from the Bronx. They sat at the table of honor with Gianni, his wife, and his children. Nonna had bought a formal gown for the occasion, and she presided over the event like a queen mother. Nonno refused to be impressed, and at one point he asked Gina how much she thought the whole thing cost. Enough to send her to college, she thought, but she didn't say it. She only said she had no idea, but it must have cost a lot.

There was live music and dancing and then a surprise. With a wireless microphone Gianni strolled out onto the floor as the band introduced a popular song that had been written for Frank Sinatra. It was called "My Way."

"*Che Dio ci protegga*," Nonno said. "He's going to sing it."

"He thinks he's Frank Sinatra," Gina said.

"Where did he ever get that idea?"

"I don't know." She believed he had gotten it from being praised for everything he did, and if she had said it, Nonno would have agreed with her. But she didn't say it.

People stopped talking and clattering their tableware when her father began singing. His vocal style and his body language closely imitated Sinatra, and he didn't have a bad voice. The problem was, he wasn't Sinatra, but there in front of an audience he thought he was.

When he finished the song people applauded, and that encouraged him to sing another, "New York, New York." And then another.

He kept singing even after people resumed talking and applauded only to be polite.

"He doesn't know when to stop," Nonno said.

Gina understood this remark as having implications beyond the present situation, and she could see how it applied to other things her father did.

When he finally did stop and returned to their table, Nonna said: "You were wonderful!"

"Thanks," her father said, glowing in triumph. Without asking what Nonno thought about his performance, he sat down between Nonna and Assunta, and he gazed out at the people dancing with a look of contentment.

In retrospect, Gina was glad she hadn't said or done anything to puncture her father's happy bubble because not long after that party his life began to go downhill.

When she woke up the next morning the first thing Gina did was check her phone for a message. But there was no message, so she went downstairs and joined Colman in the kitchen, where he was sitting at the table on his phone, evidently talking with Ron.

As she waited for him to finish the conversation she noticed that the cap on the spout of the teapot was open and she compulsively closed it, wondering if Colman had left it open on purpose as he sometimes did to tease her. It might have been his way of assuring her that no matter what happened, nothing would change between them.

She went over to the counter and poured herself a mug of coffee from the hourglass coffee maker, adding some cream to lighten it, and then sitting down at the table.

After ending the call Colman said: "Marisol has a Facebook page. The computer geek found it. Ron has a list of her virtual friends."

"Did he tell you how many there are?"

"Yeah. He said there are eighty-seven names."

"That's a lot of friends."

"It's more than I have. And he said it's hard to narrow the list because they all pretend to be something they aren't."

"Well, what does Marisol pretend to be?"

"She pretends to be a boy in college looking for action. She goes by the name of Mario."

"I might have guessed she'd pretend to be a boy, but I never would have guessed she'd be looking for action."

"Why would she pretend to be a boy?"

"Because Eileen didn't want her to be a tomboy."

"She's rebelling against Eileen?"

"Yeah, I think she is, God bless her. I never rebelled," Gina said. "I probably should have."

"Against your father?"

"Against the role he made me play."

"But someone had to play it."

"So an angel of the Lord designated me?"

"Whether or not it came from an angel, it came from on high," Colman said, smiling.

Returning to the subject, Gina said: "If she's looking for action, she might have been lured by the promise of action."

"What kind of action?"

"I don't know. I hate to think." Gina imagined the possibilities, which ranged from alcohol to drugs to sex. As far as she knew, the girl had no experience with alcohol, drugs, or sex, so she had no idea what she might be getting into.

"At least there were no pictures of her," Colman said.

"There weren't? Thank God. But don't they all post pictures of themselves?"

"I guess they do. But since she was pretending to be a boy, she couldn't post a picture of herself."

Gina reflected. "Well, what if she was lured by a girl looking for action? How would the girl feel when she found out that Marisol was a girl?"

"She'd be disappointed—unless she was gay."

"Oh, this is getting too complicated. Let's go back to our original idea that someone lured her with the hope of finding her birth mother."

"I'm already there," Colman said. "I asked Ron to have his geek search the messages on Facebook for the key words 'mother,' 'Honduras,' and 'San Pedro.' He'll follow any trail that has those words in it."

"Okay. Have you eaten anything?"

"I had a bagel. They're on the counter."

It was their tradition to have bagels every Friday, and Colman went out and got them early in the morning. Marisol liked the mini-bagels, so he would buy a half dozen of them and a half pound of cream cheese in a plastic container. Occasionally, he would also get smoked salmon, which Marisol loved.

When she opened the brown paper bag on the counter Gina saw that he had bought the usual half dozen mini-bagels, and her eyes teared up at the sight of this evidence that Colman had been hoping to find Marisol at home when he returned from the deli.

THREE

THEY WERE STILL in the kitchen when Colman's phone rang, and they both perked up, hoping it was news about Marisol. From what Gina heard of the conversation, it *was* about Marisol, but it wasn't news, it was a snag.

After a silence Colman told the caller: "That isn't necessary. I'm her uncle, and my wife is her godmother."

But the caller evidently maintained his position, and Colman finally ended the call, saying: "I'll get back to you."

"Who was that?" Gina asked.

"It was the lawyer who handled the adoption. He won't talk with us without permission from Ugo and Eileen, which he wants in writing."

"Well, at least he's willing to talk with us."

"Yeah. And he's available today."

"So I have to call Eileen and tell her what happened. I mean, I would have had to tell her anyway, but I was hoping—"

"Yeah, I know," Colman said.

She went and got her phone, which was in her pocketbook upstairs in their bedroom, and she brought it to the kitchen, where she sat down and keyed in Eileen's number. The phone at the other end rang four times, and then it went into voicemail. Gina left a message for Eileen to call her back, saying it was urgent.

"Try your brother," Colman suggested.

"My brother never answers his phone, and he never checks it." He hadn't even checked the message she left him when their father died.

"Then I think we should head there right away. I'll draw up something for them to sign, and on our way there you can try again to reach Eileen."

31

"What if Marisol comes home while we're gone?"

"We'll leave a note for her," Colman said as if that was the least of their worries.

While Gina went upstairs to dress, he went to his office and prepared a document that gave the lawyer permission to talk with them about the adoption.

They were on the Merritt Parkway, about halfway to Sudbury, when Eileen finally returned the call.

"What's happening?" Eileen asked with a note of suspicion in her voice.

"We don't know where Marisol is," Gina said. "She didn't come home yesterday, and she hasn't responded to our messages."

"You mean she's missing?"

"The police are looking for her, following leads they got from her computer."

"You shouldn't be living in that neighborhood."

Ignoring the remark, Gina said: "Colman found the lawyer who handled the adoption, and he wants a document that gives him your permission to talk with us."

"Why do you want to talk with him?"

"We think she might have gone to find her birth mother."

"Her birth mother died in a car accident."

"That's what you told her, and that's what we told her, but maybe she doesn't believe it."

"Well, I don't see how talking with that lawyer could help you find her."

Gina noticed the use of the second person pronoun, which implied that Eileen had no stake in the matter. The responsibility for finding Marisol rested entirely on Gina and Colman just as the responsibility for raising her rested entirely on them. But that was fine with Gina because she believed that the involvement of Ugo and Eileen would hinder, not help, their investigation. "He's our only source of information about Marisol's life before you adopted her, so we have to talk with him."

"Where are you now?" Eileen asked after a pause.

"We're on the Merritt Parkway. We should be at your house in about twenty minutes."

"All right. I'll wake up Ugo."

"He's not up yet?"

"Are you kidding?" Eileen laughed. "He's up all night playing on his computer, and he sleeps all day. He doesn't help me at all with the children."

"Doesn't he have to go to work?"

"No. He lost his job two months ago. He's a consultant now."

"A consultant? What does that mean?"

"It means he's unemployed."

"I'm sorry." Gina meant it, realizing that it was the first time she had felt sorry for Eileen.

After ending the call she told Colman the substance of their conversation, and then she rested her head back and closed her eyes, remembering the unconditional love that she and her sister and her brother had received from their mother.

Assunta was born in Sicily and came to America when she was almost twenty. After living with relatives in the East Nineties of Manhattan, her family moved to Throgs Neck where they lived in a recently completed low-income public housing project. From there she commuted by subway to her job as a seamstress in the Garment District. Her formal education had ended after two years of high school, but she was an avid reader and a lifelong learner, so she was informed about the world beyond her neighborhood and her workplace. In fact, she read a newspaper while riding to work and back on the subway.

When people heard she was from Sicily they couldn't believe it because she didn't match their expectation of a dark-haired, dark-eyed, dark-skinned woman. She had blond hair, blue eyes, and fair skin. With her calm, secure temperament, which radiated from her beatific smile, she could have been the model for a painting of the Madonna, and she inspired reverence in people, including Gianni Moretti, who saw her at church a few weeks after her family moved to the neighborhood. At the time Gianni didn't attend church regularly, needing Sunday morning to recover from the night before, but his mother had made him get up and go to church that Sunday, and he was rewarded for his sacrifice.

When he brought Assunta home to meet his family a few months later, his father liked her immediately, but his mother had reservations about her because she lived in the project, which was more than one level below a two-family house, but she couldn't stop her son from marrying the girl two years later. By then he was thirty-five, and he should have known what he wanted in a wife after dating so many girls.

The timing of his marriage was opportune because the family that rented the other half of the house had decided to get out of the Bronx and advance to Westchester, which enabled Gianni to have his own place and still enjoy the benefits of living with his parents. For his bride those benefits as well as the boundaries between the two households might not have been so clear. She had to live under the dominion of her mother-in-law, who had very definite ideas about how a house should be run.

Within two years of their marriage Assunta was pregnant, and Gianni and his parents were hoping it would be a boy to carry on the family name. But it was a girl, and luckily Gina had no idea how disappointed they all were, except Assunta, who considered her a blessing. At that point Assunta stopped working outside the home and devoted herself to raising her child, so Gina had a full-time mother who loved her.

Two years later Assunta was pregnant again, and again Gianni and his parents were hoping it would be a boy. But again it was a girl, and again they were all disappointed, except Assunta, who considered Leonora another blessing. Though she was only two at the time, Gina could feel her mother's happiness, and that made her happy.

Italian was spoken in both households because her mother and her grandparents had limited English, so as a young child Gina could understand conversations between her grandmother and her mother. Their conversations were usually in the kitchen, where her mother spent a lot of her time. Though her mother had been living in the house for at least five years, Nonna was still telling her how to do things and criticizing her for not doing things the right way. Among the scenes in the kitchen, Gina remembered one in particular. Her mother was cooking a red sauce that she had learned to make from her own mother, and Nonna barged into the kitchen, picked up a spoon, tasted the sauce, and spat it out saying: *"Mio figlio non dovrebbe mangiare questa spazzatura siciliana!"*

"Gianni likes this sauce," her mother said calmly.

"If he does, then you've ruined him. After eating your Sicilian garbage, he doesn't remember the taste of good cooking."

"Has he ever complained about my cooking?"

"No. He hasn't. But he should complain."

Her mother didn't respond to that. She only walked over to the stove and tasted the sauce and nodded in satisfaction. It was as if her mother had an inner peace that nothing from the outside world could disturb. It might have come from her faith in God, or it might have come from her love for other people. Wherever it came from, Gina could always rely on it being there. And she could feel it building inside of her.

It was there when that boy on the playground called her a "guinea." She knew what the name meant, and she was hurt by it, but she wasn't hurt enough to feel the need to retaliate. If anything, she felt sorry for the boy, who must have felt a need to insult her.

Gina was on her mother's side when Nonna complained about not having a grandson, ignoring the fact that Nonna herself had given birth to five girls before she finally had a boy. To deflect responsibility for what she was saying, she framed the issue in terms of what her son wanted, rather than what she wanted, saying: *"Mio figlio ha abbastanza figlie. Dovrebbe avere un figlio."*

"If God wants me to have a boy," her mother said serenely, "then it will happen."

By the time it did happen Gina was seven, and Leonora was five. And seeing how drastically things changed with the birth of her brother, Gina felt lucky to have had those years when her mother had time for her. From the very beginning Ugo demanded so much attention that her mother barely had time for anything else, but instead of helping, her grandmother only made things worse by interfering with her mother's efforts to discipline Ugo. Since her father let Ugo get away with anything, her mother's only ally was her grandfather, who after hearing that Ugo had done something outrageous muttered that he needed a kick in the ass. But her grandfather never administered a punishment, which made Gina wonder years later if it had all started with her grandfather, who had failed to discipline his own son.

Gina responded to the situation by doing everything she could to help her mother, which included playing with Leonora and assisting with the preparation of dinner. It was after the arrival of Ugo that she formed a strong bond with her sister, who like her realized that their mother was fully occupied with their brother. As they advanced through elementary school they saw how their grandmother and their father spoiled Ugo, and they sympathized with their mother.

Since she hadn't finished high school, Assunta was determined that her children should get high school diplomas. She was also determined that they should have a Catholic education all the way through college, so when Gina completed eighth grade at St. Frances de Chantal, Assunta wanted to enroll her in Preston High School, a Catholic school for girls in Throgs Neck, within walking distance from their house.

But Gianni opposed the idea, and it caused a major argument, which Gina overheard from her bedroom.

"*Quella scuola costa un sacco di soldi,*" Gianni said.

"It's an excellent school," Assunta said. "It's worth the money."

"It's no better than the public high school."

"It's a lot better. And it'll give Gina a Catholic education."

"She already got a Catholic education at St. Frances."

"She needs to continue that education. And Preston has very good teachers. They all have college degrees."

"So do the teachers at the public high school. And that's free."

"It's not free. You pay taxes for it."

"Yeah, I know. And if she didn't go to the public school I'd still have to pay taxes for it, but on top of that I'd have to pay for this school."

"If Gina does well, she might get a scholarship."

"Even if she did, we'd have to pay for the first year."

"We'll find the money."

"We will? Where?"

"We can find ways to cut our expenses," Assunta said, "and Gina can get a part-time job."

"She's only a kid. Who would hire her?"

There was a pause. "Carlo might hire her. He needs someone to help with customers."

"If he needs help, he'll hire someone from his own family."

"Then what about your office?"

"If they needed help, they wouldn't hire a kid with only an eighth-grade education."

"That's my whole point. To get a good job, you need to have a good education."

"She'll get a good enough education at the public school. I mean, she's a girl, so she doesn't need the kind of education that a boy needs."

There was a longer pause. "I want her to have a good Catholic education all the way through college, and if we can't find another way to pay for it, I'll go back to work."

"You have three kids. You can't go back to work."

"Then we'll have to find another way to pay for it," Assunta said calmly, "but our daughter is going to Preston."

Gina got a scholarship after her first semester at Preston, and from then on her father only had to pay half of the tuition. But her parents had the same discussion two years later when it was time for her sister to start high school. Her mother made the same arguments, only this time she had the fact that Gina had gotten a scholarship, and her father made the same arguments, only this time he had the fact he had just started his own business, so he had no money to spare. Again their mother threatened to go back to work, and again their father wouldn't allow it. The deadlock was broken when Gina, who by then had a part-time job at Carlo's grocery store, offered to contribute all her earnings to the family, and that finally shamed their father into letting his second daughter go to Preston.

Most of the girls at Preston expected to go to college, and Gina shared this expectation, though she knew her father didn't plan to send her to college. Encouraged by her mother, she applied to several colleges, and with her excellent grades and high test scores she was accepted by all of them. After talking with the guidance counselor she decided to go to Lehman College, which had the lowest tuition and was reachable by public transportation.

When her father learned about her plan he was furious. He ranted and raved, explaining that his business wasn't yet out of the woods, so he still had no money to spare. Her mother threatened to go back to work, her father forbade it, but this time her mother defied him and took the subway to the Garment District to meet with her former employer.

But her mother never had a chance to resume working outside the home. In the medical examination required for her job, they found a tumor in her left breast, which turned out to be cancer. She had surgery and chemotherapy, which halted the spread of the disease but left the family with a heavy burden of medical expenses because her father had decided to save money by not paying for healthcare insurance. So now, instead of going to college, Gina had to work full time to help support her family.

Shortly after she started her job at the printing company she was in the kitchen with her mother helping to prepare dinner. In her faded blue dress, with a plain scarf covering her head to hide her loss of hair from the chemotherapy, her mother could have been one of the attendant women in a scene of the Crucifixion.

"*Mi dispiace tanto*," her mother said. "I stopped you from going to college."

"You didn't stop me," Gina said. "You encouraged me. And it's certainly not your fault that you got cancer."

"I feel like it's my fault. I mean, I should have taken better care of myself."

"You didn't have time to take care of yourself. You were so busy taking care of us."

"Well, after we get through this you can go to college."

"I plan to," Gina said to let her mother know she hadn't given up the dream.

At that moment Nonna came into the kitchen and asked: "Do you need any help?"

"Thanks. I have Gina. *Grazie a Dio.*"

They were making eggplant parmesan, and Gina was carefully layering the eggplant, tomato sauce, mozzarella, and parmesan cheese into a pan.

"Did you bake the eggplant?" Nonna asked.

"Yes," Assunta said. "I'm trying it that way. It's less fattening."

"You don't need to worry about your weight."

"No, I don't, but your son does. He has a pot belly."

"He doesn't have a pot belly."

"If he doesn't," Gina said, "then he's pregnant. Have you seen him lately?"

"I see him every day," her grandmother said as if she didn't like the lack of respect in Gina's comment about her father.

Gina was conscious of the fact that her respect for her father had diminished since her mother had been diagnosed with cancer. No doubt he loved her mother and needed her, but at every stage of the terrifying process he had acted as if it was happening to him—the surgery, the chemotherapy, and the after-effects. While her mother never lost her dignity, her father totally lost control and made things even worse with his histrionics.

For three years her mother's cancer went into remission, but then it returned. At the time Gina was planning to register as an evening student at Hunter College to pursue a bachelor's degree in business administration. Instead, for the next six months she spent her evenings and her weekends taking care of her mother, whose condition slowly deteriorated as the cancer spread to her bones. When the end came she was at her mother's bedside at Calvary Hospital, along with Leonora and her father. She had tried but failed to reach Ugo.

With her eyes half closed her mother gestured for Gina to lean toward her and listen to something she wanted to say. The words were barely audible but Gina understood them. Her mother said: "Promise you'll take care of your father."

"I will," Gina promised.

Now, as they turned onto the street where Ugo and Eileen lived, the news that Ugo had lost his job made Gina feel sympathy toward him, though she also felt resentment toward him because his family had given him everything and he obviously didn't appreciate the sacrifices they had made for him.

Colman parked his car in the driveway to the left of Eileen's sport utility vehicle. The front entrance of the house was used only for company, so Gina and Colman went through the garage, where there was barely enough room to get around the gigantic truck that Ugo had to have. The truck guzzled gas, so it wasn't efficient for commuting, but evidently Ugo needed to drive a big truck to assert his masculinity.

Gina and Colman climbed the stairs to the hallway, where there was a rack for hanging coats. The hallway led to the kitchen, where they found Eileen sitting at the counter with a mug of coffee in front of her. She rose to greet them, asking: "Would you like some coffee?"

"No, thanks," Gina said. She sat down on one of the bar stools at the counter, and Colman sat down next to her. "Is Ugo up?"

"Yeah, he's taking a shower."

"We need him to sign a document."

"Do you really think she went to find her birth mother?"

"We don't know what else to think, except that she could have been lured by someone who promised her friendship."

"That's more likely," Eileen said. "She had no friends when she lived with us, and it sounds like she didn't make any friends living with you."

"She has friends on Facebook," Gina said.

"But they're not real friends."

"I know they're not."

At that moment Ugo appeared. His hair was still wet from his shower, and he was wearing a white tee shirt and blue shorts. As loose as his shirt was, it revealed a belly that had grown a lot bigger since the last time Gina saw him. And his right arm was in a sling.

"What happened to your arm?" Gina asked.

"It's not my arm, it's my shoulder," Ugo said.

"Then what happened to your shoulder?"

"I have a condition."

"You mean an injury?"

"No, a condition."

"He gets a pain in his shoulder," Eileen said as if she was already tired of it, "when he moves his arm or raises it."

"It could be a torn rotator cuff," Colman said.

"That's what the doctor says it is," Ugo said. "He says it could have happened when I painted the ceiling in the powder room."

"You didn't paint it," Eileen said.

"Well, I started to paint it."

"You got as far as opening the can of paint."

There was a silence, and then Ugo asked: "What are you guys doing here?"

"Marisol is missing," Gina told him. "We don't know where she is, but we think she might have gone to find her birth mother."

Ugo shook his head, saying: "She didn't go to find her birth mother."

"We think she might have, so we want to talk with the lawyer who handled her adoption."

Ugo paused to open a box of Entenmann's donuts that was on the counter. They were glazed donuts, a dozen of them, and he carefully selected one and took a large bite of it. Munching, he asked: "What exactly do you need from us?"

"We need your permission to talk with that lawyer."

"There's no point in talking with him. The guy's an idiot."

"Maybe he is, but he could have information that would help us find Marisol."

Ugo swallowed the last of the donut and then reached for another, bringing it to his mouth in a continuous motion. "You should have watched her more closely."

"Let's not get into a pissing match," Gina said. "We need to work together on this."

"If they want to talk with him," Eileen said, "I think we should let them."

For a while Ugo munched on the donut as if it deserved his full attention, and then he said: "Do you want us to sign something?"

"Yeah," Colman said, taking a folded paper out of his pocket. "This gives the lawyer your permission to talk with us and tell us anything he knows about Marisol—"

"You mean Meredith."

"—and her antecedents."

Ugo reached for another donut.

"Save some for the kids," Eileen told him.

"Speaking of the kids," Gina said, "where are they?"

"They're downstairs playing computer games."

Gina wondered if the girls, who were now fifteen, and the boy, who was now twelve, were playing the kind of games that Marisol had played at their ages, in which the objective was to kill as many enemies as possible.

After eating a third donut Ugo picked up the document and looked at it. "You got her name wrong. It's Meredith."

"No, it isn't. She changed it back to Marisol."

"You didn't ask our permission for that."

"We didn't need your permission. She was of legal age for that purpose. And the name they used in the adoption documents was Marisol."

"If she's of legal age, then you should get her permission to talk with the lawyer."

"That's not funny," Gina said.

"It wasn't meant to be funny," Ugo said, putting the document down on the counter.

"I'll sign it," Eileen said, reaching for it.

Mustering all the sympathy she was able to feel for her brother, Gina said: "I heard you lost your job."

"Yeah. They offshored it to India, along with thousands of other jobs. You know, IBM has more employees in India than they have in America."

"There are a lot of other tech companies."

"Yeah, I know. But they're all doing the same thing. They're replacing us with wogs."

"So what are you doing?"

"I'm a consultant," Ugo said. "I know the systems, so I can help companies that use them."

"Do you have a list of contacts?"

"No. But I can build one."

Gina wondered how successful he would be at consulting because he had never worked directly with clients, and she knew from friends who were consultants that they spent more than half of their time marketing themselves.

"I've signed it," Eileen said, sliding the document across the counter. "Now, you sign it."

"Well, I don't feel like signing it."

"We don't give a damn how you feel about it. Just sign the fucking document."

Gina was startled, having never heard Eileen talk to Ugo that way. Together with other things she had said, it indicated a problem in their relationship.

Ugo reluctantly signed the document and then walked out of the kitchen in a huff.

"He's not himself," Eileen said, apologizing for him. "Losing his job was a blow to him."

"With his experience he can get another job," Gina told her.

"He says he can't get another job because they're offshoring all the jobs in his field."

"Then he should change fields. He should find an area where they're not offshoring."

"Like what?" Eileen asked.

"Like security," Colman said.

"I'll suggest that." Eileen paused and then she blurted out: "He has to get a job. We can't live on what I'm making."

For the second time Gina felt sorry for Eileen. What her brother needed was a kick in the ass, but now wasn't the time to give him one.

They were about to leave when the kids appeared from the basement.

Gina hugged them one after another and asked them how they were doing. She wasn't their godmother because Eileen had awarded that role to her aunts, but Gina loved them and had an interest in them. Face to face, she had no trouble telling the twins apart: Hailey was more open than Harper.

They went for the donuts, and while they were eating them Hailey asked: "Why didn't you bring Meredith with you?"

"She had another engagement," Gina said.

"Well, next time please bring her. I really miss her."

"Okay. We will. And you can come and visit us sometime."

"That would be great. I love the city. When I get older, I want to live there."

Gina exchanged a hug with Eileen, and then they left, going down the stairs and around the massive truck in the garage.

Before getting into the car, Colman called the lawyer, whose office was in Pleasantville. They arranged to meet there in an hour.

As they pulled out of the driveway Colman said: "Your brother wasn't helpful."

"Yeah, I know. He's never helpful."

"If Eileen hadn't ordered him to sign the document, he probably wouldn't have done it."

"I never saw her make him do something. She was always enabling him. But now that he's not the main provider, maybe things have changed."

"Well, he has to get a job. I don't think he can make a living as a consultant."

"I don't think so either. He didn't inherit our father's abilities as a salesman, and consultants have to market themselves."

"Do you think he'll really look for a job?"

"I don't know," Gina said. "He's so lazy, and I don't where he got that from. No one in our family was lazy."

At that moment Colman's phone rang, so he pulled over and answered it.

Listening to his side of the conversation, Gina couldn't tell who it was, and when the call ended she asked: "Who was that?"

"It was Ron. He said they've identified one of her friends, a guy who has a record for sexual assaults. He lives in the Bronx, so they're going to question him."

"I hope they don't find her with him."

Colman took her hand. "Yeah. I hope they find her with some guy who only wants money for information about her mother."

"Let's pray that they will," Gina said, leaning against him and trying not to think about the other possible scenarios.

FOUR

THE LAWYER'S OFFICE was on Wheeler Avenue, where they couldn't find a parking place, so they parked in a public lot and walked back to Wheeler. The office was on the second floor of a building that had a bakery cafe on the ground floor, and after making sure it was the right building, they climbed the stairs.

Stopping at the door that had the lawyer's name on it, Allen Corbett, they rang the bell and waited. It took a few minutes for the door to open, revealing a casually dressed man in his fifties with wiry gray hair and rimless glasses.

"Who are you?" the man asked, still in a position to shut the door on them.

"I'm Colman," Colman said. "And this is Gina."

"I'm Allen," the man said, stepping aside. "Please come in."

They followed him through the reception area into an office, where there was a desk and a sitting area. There were photographs of famous Yankee players on the walls.

"You're a baseball fan?" Colman said as they sat down.

"Oh, yeah. I was born and raised in the Bronx," Allen said, "and these guys were my heroes."

"Well, it looks like we made a good acquisition in Tanaka, but I don't know about the other pitchers.

Gina listened patiently while they analyzed the merits of the Yankee starting pitchers. Her father hadn't been a baseball fan, so she hadn't picked up from him an interest in the sport, but having been born and raised in the Bronx, she understood how important the local team was to guys from the borough.

"Okay," Colman said as if they had settled the issue of Yankee pitching, "we came here to talk with you about Marisol Moretti."

46

"Do you have permission from her parents for me to talk with you?"

"I have it right here." At that point Colman took the folded paper out of his pocket and handed it to the lawyer.

Allen examined it carefully, and then he said: "Okay. Let's talk."

"The first thing I need to know," Colman said, "is the name of the orphanage where the girl was living at the time of her adoption. I looked through the papers her adoptive mother gave me, and I couldn't find it."

"Before we get into it," Allen said, "could you tell me what interest you have in the girl?"

"I told you on the phone. I'm her uncle."

"And I'm her godmother," Gina said.

"But why aren't her adoptive parents trying to find her?"

"She doesn't live with them," Colman said. "She lives with us."

"They gave up on her four years ago," Gina said, "and they handed her over to us."

"I'm not surprised," Allen said.

"Why aren't you surprised?"

"I have a lot of experience handling adoptions, and I've seen a lot of different cases. But this one was weird." The lawyer paused. "I mean, usually when couples adopt a child they both want to have children. But from what I saw of that couple, only the woman wanted to have children. The man didn't want to have them."

"You saw that?"

"Yeah. I also saw that the woman wanted the kind of child that it's almost impossible to find—a white baby, whose parents had no vices and no health problems."

"So how did they happen to adopt Marisol?" Colman asked.

"I found a baby for them," Allen said, leaning back in his chair. "Its parents had been killed in a car accident. They had no vices and no health problems. And they had no extended family to raise the baby. It was a perfect situation."

"Why didn't they adopt it?" Gina asked.

"When they saw the baby they didn't want it."

"Why not?" Colman asked.

"It wasn't white."

"But Marisol wasn't white, so why did they adopt her?"

"Compared with that baby, she probably looked white to them. But I warned them about her," Allen said. "I told them her mother was a drug addict and a prostitute, and that her father might have been a dealer and a pimp. So it wasn't a situation where the parents had no vices and no health problems."

"They told Marisol that her mother died in a car accident."

Allen shook his head. "The mother of the baby they didn't want was the one who died in a car accident. For all I know, the mother of this girl is still alive."

"If her mother was alive at the time of the adoption," Colman said, "you must have gotten her permission for it."

"Oh, yeah. I did. You should have found that document among the papers."

"I didn't find it. And if it *had* been among the papers, I would have found it."

"Then the adoptive mother must have destroyed it."

"Maybe she didn't want Marisol to find it."

"That makes sense. If she told the kid her mother died in a car accident," Allen said wryly, "it would have been embarrassing if the kid found a document signed by her mother at the time of her adoption."

"It would have been," Gina said.

"I also warned them about the problems of adopting a kid who was almost seven. At that age kids are very far along in their development, and it's much harder than it is with babies to mold them into what you want."

"It sounds like you knew they'd try to mold her into what they wanted."

"All parents do that to some extent," Allen said. "But with them it was obvious. They wanted a kid who fit their image of a family living in Sudbury."

"You know Sudbury?"

Allen nodded. "It's not a multicultural community."

"It's not the Bronx," Colman agreed.

"I've had other clients from there. I hate to generalize, but they all want the same thing—a white baby, whose parents had no vices and no health problems."

"If you knew she wasn't what they wanted," Gina asked after a moment, "why did you let them adopt her?"

"I'm only a lawyer, not a family counselor. But at one point I did tell them that if they wanted to proceed with the adoption, they'd have to find another lawyer."

"What did they say?"

"They said they'd find another lawyer. And since I knew they'd be shafted by another lawyer, I finally agreed to represent them."

"Can we have a copy of the document signed by her mother?" Colman asked.

"Yeah, sure. And you can have a copy of the document that gives the name of the orphanage where the kid was living at the time of the adoption. It sounds like her adoptive mother destroyed that too."

"She evidently did because I didn't find it."

Allen sighed. "I can understand why adoptive parents don't want their kids to find their birth mothers, but I don't think they should wipe out the trail. The kids may have good reasons for wanting to find their birth mothers. For example, to learn if they have an inheritable disease. But it's not unusual for adoptive parents to destroy documents that might lead kids to their birth mothers. So their kids come to me looking for information."

"Are you legally allowed to give it to them?" Colman asked.

"That's a good question. And the answer is, I ask the kids to get their parents to give me permission to talk with them, as I did with you."

"But you might not need permission from the parents to talk with their kids."

"Whether or not I need it," Allen said, "I want the kids to talk with their parents. I don't want them going behind their parents' backs."

"I understand," Gina said. "I wish Marisol had talked with us."

"I wonder why she didn't. You're not her parents, so you don't have a reason to stop her from finding her birth mother."

"I guess she didn't trust us enough to talk with us."

"I know what that's like," Allen said. "I have kids of my own, and they get into trouble doing things that if they'd talked with me in advance, they wouldn't have done."

"From my experience," Colman said, "that's the only way they learn. I mean, from getting into trouble. Whatever you tell them in advance, they don't believe it."

"Then why do we try to stop them from getting into trouble?" Gina asked.

"I don't know. I guess so when they do get into trouble, at least we can feel we tried to stop them."

"Well, you have a challenge," Allen said. "This poor kid was abandoned by her birth mother, and then she was abandoned by her adoptive mother. That's a double whammy."

"We know," Gina said, "but we were hoping we could help her rise above what happened to her."

"We're still hoping," Colman said. "We're going to find her, and we're going to help her rise above it."

"Maybe she'll learn from this experience," Allen said.

"I hope so," Gina said. "I hope she realizes that whatever she's looking for, she already has it."

Colman reached over and took her hand.

Allen made copies of the two documents, and he didn't charge for his time, muttering that it was penance for not stopping the adoption.

On the trip back to Yonkers she wondered when she should contact Leonora and tell her what had happened. She could expect to get comfort from Leonora, but she didn't want to lay a burden on her sister, especially since it was still possible that Marisol would show up that evening.

Leonora inherited her mother's blond hair, blue eyes, and fair skin, which could have been advantageous for her in terms of sibling competition for resources. Her resemblance to her mother could have influenced her father to favor her, but it seemed to have the opposite effect. It was as if Gianni resented her for having her mother's physical features, maybe because she challenged the uniqueness of the woman he had chosen to be his wife. For some reason, he was extremely hard on Leonora from the beginning, and though he wasn't easy on Gina, he seemed to favor her. And Leonora enjoyed no special consideration from Nonna, who might have seen her as a reminder of her losing campaign against Assunta—now there were two Sicilians in the house.

Ignoring her husband and her mother-in-law, Assunta gave her second baby the same loving care she had given her first baby, and even at the age of two Gina sensed her fairness and had no negative feelings toward the person who had ended her reign as an only child. In fact, she loved her baby sister, and as soon as she was old enough she helped her mother take care of her. Their bond was sealed with the birth of Ugo when Gina was seven and Leonora was five because they realized that from that point on neither of them would get any attention. To their father, Ugo, as the male who would carry on the family name, was the only child who mattered, and to their grandmother, Ugo, as the reincarnation of her pride and joy, was the only grandchild who mattered. And though their mother tried to continue giving equal attention to all her children, Ugo demanded so much attention that she had little time for the girls.

They were close enough in age so that they could play with the same friends in the neighborhood, and at school they were only two grades apart, which made it easy for Gina to help Leonora in subjects that she had trouble with. Leonora was smart, but though she embraced the social side of school, she rejected the academic side. Like her mother she preferred to teach herself, and it didn't take her long to develop her own ideas, which invariably conflicted with her father's ideas. A memorable argument between them occurred the year before she started high school while Leonora was being prepared for Confirmation. They were at the dinner table when Leonora said: "I don't see why I have to go to those classes. I have enough classes in school."

"You have to learn the doctrine of our church," her father said.

"I know what I believe, and that's enough. I don't have to learn all those stupid details."

"They're not stupid details. They're things that as a good Catholic you should know."

"Well, I'll bet you don't know them. I'll bet you couldn't pass a test on them."

"I might be rusty on some of them," her father admitted. "But when I was your age, I learned them. And you're going to learn them."

Later, when they had escaped to the privacy of the bedroom they shared, Leonora said: "He's full of bullshit. He pretends to be religious because he goes to church. And even there I've seen him doze off during the homilies."

"Well, the homilies can be boring," Gina said, not in defense of their father but in support of the truth.

"They're not as boring as those classes."

"You're almost done with them."

"Yeah, I know. But I'm not done with *him*. I'm going to have to live with him at least until I finish high school."

When she was in high school Leonora developed her own set of friends, including a girl whose older brother had served in Vietnam. The brother, who had been drafted into the army at the age of nineteen, had seen enough of war to make him a pacifist, and he freely shared his views with his younger sister and her friends. Saigon had fallen to the communists a week earlier, and television commentators were busy debating the significance of what looked like a defeat for America. Inevitably, the subject came up at the dinner table when Gianni said: "We should have kept fighting. If we'd thrown everything we had into that war, we would have beaten the communists, just like we beat the Nazis."

"We never should have gotten involved there," Leonora said.

"You mean we should have just let the communists take over that country?"

"It's their country, and they should decide who runs it."

"You don't know what you're talking about. They don't have a democracy like we do, so war is the only way of deciding who runs the country."

"Then we should have let them fight their own war. We shouldn't have sent our men there."

"If we'd let them fight their own war, the communists would have won years ago. They had the support of Russia and China."

"The communists have won now, so what did we accomplish?"

"We accomplished a lot. We showed them we weren't going to let them take over the world."

"I think we showed them we can be beaten."

"It's unpatriotic to talk that way," Gianni said, beginning to get angry. "You should respect your country."

"How can I respect a country that drafted only poor people and sent them to war?"

"We didn't draft only poor people. Every young man had a draft number."

"But if you were rich, you could go to college and defer being drafted. So it was the poor people who got drafted."

"Where did you get that information?"

"I got it from my friend's older brother. He spent a year in Vietnam."

"Only a year? And that makes her brother an expert? I spent three years in Italy, and I don't consider myself an expert."

"That was a different war," Leonora said.

"How was it different?" Gianni asked, humoring her.

"It had a purpose."

"Yes, it did. And the war in Vietnam had a purpose—to stop the communists."

"But it didn't stop the communists. At least your war stopped the Nazis."

That was as close as they got to a meeting of minds. And for a while they declared a truce on this issue. But there were always more issues, with Leonora and her father on opposite sides.

Then, in Leonora's senior year in high school, they had an argument not about a public issue but about Leonora's personal behavior. She was dating a boy who went to Fordham. He was twenty, and he had a car, which he used to take Leonora to places outside of the neighborhood. At that time the drinking age in New York was still eighteen, and often they went to parties where significant amounts of alcohol were consumed. Leonora was supposed to be home by midnight, but she didn't always meet this deadline, and one time when she was very late her father was waiting for her, ready to confront her. Since they were shouting, and since the family lived on one floor, Gina was able to hear them from her bed.

"*Sai che ora è?*" her father roared.

"Yes. It's quarter of two," Leonora said defiantly.

"You're supposed to be home by twelve."

"I know. But we got caught in traffic."

"Don't lie to me. You didn't get caught in traffic for almost two hours."

"Well, I was having fun, and I lost track of the time."

"You were having fun? What were you doing?"

"Talking with people, laughing with them."

"Are you sure you weren't doing anything else?"

"You mean like having sex with Kieron?"

"Don't get smart with me, young lady."

"I wasn't getting smart with you. I only said what you were thinking."

"I wasn't thinking that," her father said indignantly.

"Don't lie to me," Leonora said, imitating him.

At that point there was the sound of a palm smacking a cheek.

There was a pause, and then Leonora said: "That's what your generation always does when you lose an argument. You resort to violence."

"You're grounded for a month. Do you understand?"

"*Capisco perfettamente,*" Leonora said.

And then there was silence.

A few minutes later Leonora came into their bedroom and began undressing in the dark.

"Are you all right?" Gina asked.

"Yeah, I'm all right," Leonora sighed. "I guess you heard us."

"I heard every word. And I'm on your side, but—"

"I know. I shouldn't talk to papa that way."

"I understand your feelings," Gina said, "but I also understand *his* feelings."

"You mean his fear that his daughter will get pregnant."

"Yeah, or get killed in a car accident."

"Okay. So he has feelings. But he should trust me. I wouldn't get into a car with a guy who's had too much to drink. And I wouldn't have unprotected sex."

The last remark made Gina wonder if Leonora hadn't told her about something because as far as she knew, her sister was still a virgin.

"Hey, I didn't mean I'm having protected sex. But the more he thinks I am having sex, the more I want to have it. Does that make any sense?"

"Yeah, it does. But please don't do something just because he doesn't want you to."

"Don't worry. I won't."

When Leonora graduated from high school their father's business was flourishing so there was no pressure for her to go to work and contribute money to the family. But she didn't want to go to college, she wanted to get a job and earn money and gain independence. By then they had moved to the house on Palmer Road, so she looked for a job in Yonkers and found one as a waitress in an Irish pub on McLean Avenue. She opened her own bank account and began saving money with the goal of accumulating enough for the deposit and the advance rent on her own apartment.

She was still living at home when Gianni had his party at the Waldorf Astoria, so she had to attend, but she was buffered from her father by her mother at the head table, so she saved her remarks for Gina after they got home. They agreed that their father's performance reflected his need always to be the center of attention.

Leonora had enough money to move out of the house, and she was looking at possible apartments in Yonkers when their mother died, so she stayed for Gina, who was left with the responsibility of making arrangements for the funeral and handling all the related matters. Gina welcomed her support, but she didn't want her sister to miss the opportunity to gain her independence, and she assured her that it would be all right if she moved out. She even told her about their mother's last words, which had designated Gina as the one who should take care of their father.

Still, Leonora didn't move out until after a final blow-up with her father. Gianni went to pieces after losing his wife, and he was barely able to perform the necessary daily functions. He didn't go to work, he stayed in the house, and he prowled around looking for someone to blame for his loss. Gina had taken an unpaid vacation from her job to be there for him, and Leonora didn't go to work until four, so they were both there, while Ugo was at school. It was only a matter of time before Gianni focused his attention on Leonora, whose resemblance to her mother aroused in him an uncontrollable rage over the fact that his beloved wife was dead and his rebellious daughter was alive. It didn't help that he had been drinking black Sambuca for the past few hours.

"I thought you were going to move out," he told her.

"I was going to move out," Leonora said. "But I'm staying for a while to help Gina."

"Help her with what?"

"Help her with you."

"I don't need your help. So you can move out."

"It's not all about you, papa. I don't want to desert my sister."

"Since when did you worry about deserting people?"

"I've always worried about it."

"No, you haven't. You don't care about the family. You only care about yourself."

"I care about the family. But I don't care about the family so much that I don't care what happens to me. And unlike you, I might not have a family to take care of me."

"If you cared at all about the family, you wouldn't have worried your mother to death."

"Now, wait a minute," Leonora said, as angry as Gina had ever seen her. "Are you blaming me for mama's death?"

"I'm only saying that if you hadn't caused her so much stress, she might not have gotten cancer."

"It's not right for you to say that," Gina said, intervening. "If anyone caused her stress, it was you."

"How did I cause your mother stress?"

"By not being happy with what you had. By trying to make more money than we needed. By buying this house. And by trying to be Frank Sinatra."

Her father looked at her as if he didn't recognize her. "I can't believe you'd say such things about your father."

"I only said them to stop you from hurting Leonora."

"How was I hurting Leonora?"

"By blaming her for our mother's death."

"I wasn't blaming her."

"Yes, you were," Leonora said. "You said I worried my mother to death."

"Well, I didn't mean that."

"You sounded like you meant it."

"Even if you didn't mean it," Gina said, "I think you should tell Leonora you're sorry."

"You think I should tell my daughter I'm sorry?"

"Yeah, I do. We've all suffered a terrible loss, and we should support each other in our grief. We shouldn't hurt each other."

"I didn't hurt her."

"You did hurt me."

There was a long silence.

And then, before leaving the room, their father muttered: "You don't care about me."

When he was out of hearing range Gina and Leonora discussed what had happened. They agreed that it would be best if Leonora proceeded with her plan to move out, and within a month she was living in a one-bedroom apartment on Lake Avenue in Yonkers.

By then Gina had a car, which she had leased after they had moved to Palmer Road. Since she could no longer take the subway to work she needed the car to go to the Yonkers train station and commute to Manhattan from there. She also needed the car for shopping because she couldn't walk to any stores from where they lived. And now she needed it to visit her sister.

It wasn't long before Leonora developed a serious relationship with a guy who drove a bus for a private company whose main business was running expresses into and out of Manhattan for people who didn't live near train stations. His name was Jerry, he was twenty-six, and he had a degree in business from Iona, but he hadn't been able to find a job that paid as well as the one from which he had earned enough to pay for college, so he kept driving a bus. He lived in an apartment on McLean Avenue, and they had met in the pub where Leonora worked. Unlike her father, he was patient and kind and considerate.

At the end of a year, when her lease was up, Leonora moved in with him, and within a year she was pregnant. They were married in a rush ceremony at Sacred Heart Church in Yonkers, where Jerry's family were parishioners. Leonora's condition didn't show yet, so there were no problems, and even her father didn't make an issue of the fact that her first baby, Darcy, was born about seven months after their wedding. Leonora had told him the baby was premature, and at least he pretended to believe it.

Three years later her second baby, Selma, was born. By then they had bought a house in the Bryn Mawr neighborhood of Yonkers. Jerry was making enough money so that Leonora, following the model of her mother, could stay at home and raise her children.

Lenora and her father had made peace. His only complaint about her was that she hadn't yet given him a grandson.

When they got to Yonkers they went directly to the police station, where they met in an office with Ron and his partner. It was a small office, but there was nowhere else for them to meet at the station. Ron sat behind a metal desk while Emilio sat on the edge of it, dangling his legs and tapping out a Latin rhythm with his heels against the side of it, until Ron gave him a look that stopped him.

Colman gave Ron the documents he had gotten from the lawyer, and Ron recounted how they had questioned the guy who had a record for sexual assaults.

"I don't think he's the one," Ron said. "At least I know he never met the girl face to face."

"How do you know?" Colman asked.

"He thinks she's a boy."

"Oh, yeah. Well, that could help you filter the list. I mean, you can eliminate people who think she's a boy."

"We're already doing that."

"How do you know if they think she's a boy?" Gina asked.

"We ask them a series of questions," Emilio said, "in which they have to use the masculine or feminine pronoun."

"You could have been a teacher," Rod said.

"That's what my mother wanted me to be, but it wasn't what I wanted to be."

"Well, God bless you for wanting to be a cop."

"So you're filtering out people who think she's a boy," Colman resumed. "How small is the list now?"

"We're down to twenty-two suspects," Emilio said, "and half of them live in the New York area."

"Do any of them live in Honduras?"

"Not that we can tell. But a few of them live in Miami."

"At the same time," Colman said, "we should try to find the mother. We have her name now."

"We're assuming she still lives in San Pedro Sula," Gina said.

"So we'll have to contact the police there," Ron said.

"They're not known for being helpful," Emilio said. "They're so busy fighting the drug gangs, they can't be bothered with ordinary crimes."

"The problem is, we have no evidence that a crime has been committed. We only have a missing person."

"Do you think it would help if I went there to work with the police?" Colman asked.

"I think it would. But don't buy a plane ticket yet. We're still checking the girl's friends on Facebook, and we could find out that she stayed in New York."

"I hope she did," Gina said. "But I have a feeling she's on her way to Honduras."

"Then we'll contact the police in San Pedro and tell them what we know so far."

"And we'll get ready to go there," Colman said.

Gina was ready to go there now, but she knew she had to let Ron and Emilio continue their process. It wouldn't help for her to get ahead of them, so she had to be patient, though it was hard because she was afraid that the longer it took them to find Marisol, the more damage would be done to her.

FIVE

THAT EVENING, WHEN Gina had finished cleaning up after dinner, she joined Colman in his office. He was trying to get a phone number for the orphanage in San Pedro Sula where Marisol was living at the time of her adoption. Gina sat down on the sofa where over the years so many people had poured their hearts out to Colman, seeking his help. If they couldn't pay him, which was often the case, he didn't charge them for his services. He lived on the income he received from preparing wills and closing purchases of homes for people who could afford to pay him. Once, early in their relationship, after she told him how much she admired his commitment to a mission, he responded by telling her how much he admired *her* commitment to a mission, and when she asked him what mission, he said her family, which she had never thought of as a mission. Now, as she heard him talking in Spanish at long distance, she felt they were united in a mission, and more than anything in the world it gave her the confidence she needed to deal with the situation.

"At least someone answered the phone," Colman told her while he waited.

Gina held her breath.

"*Hola? Habla Colman Hayes. Soy abogado, y estoy buscando a una chica—*" He paused, listened, and then repeated: "*Soy abogado, y estoy buscando a una chica que vivía en tu orfanato hace once años. Se llama Marisol.*"

Gina listened, hoping that the person he was talking with remembered the girl. Eleven years was a long time, but the orphanage sounded Catholic, and maybe the person was one of those nuns who never forgot anything.

After about a half hour Colman ended the call. "That was Sister

Eugenia. She remembered Marisol. She said it was unusual for a girl her age to be adopted."

"Did she know anything about the mother?"

"She said the mother was alive at the time of the adoption."

"We already knew that. Did she know anything else about her?"

"She said the mother was on the street about five years ago, working as a prostitute. She referred her to a lay worker whose mission was to rehabilitate women in that situation. But the mother went back to working on the street, and that was the last thing the sister knew about her."

"Did she tell you how the girl happened to be placed in the orphanage?"

"She was found on the street, abandoned by her mother. She was three years old."

"So why wasn't she adopted when she was younger?"

"The sister said there was something about her that made people have second thoughts. And when she was older she strongly resisted being adopted, maybe because she was hoping that her mother would come and get her."

"But she didn't resist being adopted by Ugo and Eileen?"

"No. She didn't. The sister said that by then she might have given up hope that her mother would come and get her."

"Did the sister remember Ugo and Eileen?"

"Oh, yeah, and she remembered having doubts about them."

"Doubts? What kind of doubts?"

"She had doubts about their reasons for adopting," Colman said. "But she thought it was the girl's last chance, and Marisol didn't resist being adopted by them, as she did with the previous couples."

"Well, I wonder what would have happened to her if she hadn't been adopted."

"I asked the sister, and she said she would have been placed as a servant in a rich family."

"That wouldn't have been the worst thing," Gina said.

"Yeah, I agree. The worst thing would have been to end up like her mother."

"We don't know how her mother ended up."

"No, we don't. But we can guess."

"Do you think it's possible," Gina asked, "that someone she met online really knows where her mother is?"

"It's possible. So if her mother's still alive, we have to find her. And the last person to see her alive was the lay worker who tried to rehabilitate her."

"Did you get a phone number?"

"Yeah. I was going to try it after I told you what I learned from the sister."

"Then go ahead and try it." Gina waited tensely while he keyed the numbers into his phone.

After a while he ended the call, shaking his head. "It's out of service. So I only have the address of where she was."

"We can ask the police to track her down."

"I'll give Ron this information."

"Okay," Gina said, though she believed it was a higher priority for the police to keep trying to find the person who had lured the girl wherever she had gone. If that trail led to San Pedro Sula, then they could track down the lay worker.

The next morning she left for work at eighty thirty as usual even though she didn't work on Saturdays unless they needed extra help. She intended to ask for a week off so she would be available to help Colman and the police look for Marisol, and she thought it would be better to ask in person than over the phone. She worked in a high-end kitchen store at Ridge Hill, a new shopping center in Yonkers. It had several other high-end stores as well as a variety of popular restaurants, and it was still in the development stage, but the kitchen store was doing well, being the only unit in southern Westchester of a well-regarded national chain. This job, which she had held for almost two years, gave her more responsibility and paid her a higher salary than the job in the kitchen department of Macy's, where she had worked for seven years following the demise of her father's business.

Ridge Hill was only about fifteen minutes from her house, depending on traffic. From Nodine Hill she got onto Nepperhan

Avenue and drove north to Old Nepperhan Avenue, then over to Saw Mill River Road, then east on Tuckahoe Road, and again north on Ridge Hill Boulevard, which led to the shopping center. It was an easy commute, and by now she could follow this route without thinking about it—a good thing because this morning her mind was on San Pedro Sula. From what she had heard, she imagined a city that was worse than any of the bad areas that she had seen in the New York area, with gangs roaming the blighted streets. She couldn't bear to think of Marisol wandering around in such a place, looking for her mother.

Gina parked her car in an area designated for employees and walked into the store, which on weekdays was open to the public from ten in the morning to nine at night. Except during the holiday season her regular hours were nine to five. Her primary function was to manage inventory and provide information to buyers at the chain's headquarters, so she had a desk in the back office, but she was also expected to spend time dealing with customers not only to sell products to them but also to get feedback from them, which she could pass on to the buyers. She liked both aspects of her job, which complemented each other.

The store manager, Vicki, was already in the other private office, holding a giant coffee mug emblazoned with the logo of the Yankees. She was a rangy young woman, on her way up the hierarchical ladder of the corporation, aiming at the next rung of regional manager. She was a good boss, and she was smart enough to know that without happy, productive employees she would never advance beyond her present level.

"Have you got a minute?" Gina asked.

"Yeah, sure," Vicki said, gazing at her attentively. "You don't look good. What's happening?"

"I need to take a week off. My goddaughter is missing, and we're trying to find her."

"Oh, my God. How long has she been missing?"

"Since Thursday evening. We think she was going to meet someone, but we don't know who and we don't know where."

"She didn't leave a note or anything?"

"No. She just took off."

Vicki shook her head with sympathy. "After all you did for that poor child."

"I feel I didn't do enough for her," Gina said. "I feel that if only I'd done more for her, she wouldn't have gone without even leaving a note."

"It's not your fault. It's the fault of the people who had her before you. How old was she when she came to live with you?"

"Fourteen."

"And how old is she now?"

"She's eighteen."

"So you've had her only four years. That's not enough to make a difference with a kid who was abandoned twice."

"Well, I hope we'll have another chance with her. But we have to find her, and I need time off to help my husband and the police look for her."

"Then take an early vacation, starting today. Take as long as you need."

"Thanks. I really appreciate it."

Vicki made a gesture with her hand that meant that it was the least she could do for a good employee, and then she lifted the coffee mug.

Everything about Ugo was difficult, beginning with his birth, which took several hours longer than the births of his sisters. It was as if he didn't want to leave the comfort and security of his mother's womb, and he came into the world kicking and screaming.

He was difficult to nurse. He had an insatiable appetite for milk, and even after he had sucked his mother dry he refused to let go of her sore nipples. To supplement her own resources Assunta tried giving him milk from a bottle, but he not only rejected it, he threw it on the floor, and he screamed as if he had been critically injured.

Unlike most babies, he rarely slept, and while he was awake he demanded that his mother hold him. At times when Assunta had something else to do, she handed him to Gina, but he spat at her and once he threw up on her.

"Yuck," she cried, handing the baby back to their mother. "He did that deliberately."

"No, he didn't," Assunta told her, soothing Ugo. "He couldn't help it."

Gina wasn't convinced that he couldn't help throwing up on her, or that he couldn't help doing the other things he did to disturb the peace.

Assunta did get help from Nonna, who could hold Ugo at least for a while before he started pushing off from her. Nonna said she understood his behavior because he was like his father, and she tolerated whatever he did, just as she had tolerated whatever her own baby boy did, repeating the cycle.

As soon as Ugo could toddle he was in motion continuously, stopping only to break something. By then Gina had homework to do, and she had a hard time concentrating with all the noise her brother made.

Things got worse when Ugo was old enough to play with toys. His favorite toy was a fire engine, which he drove around making a noise like its siren. Day and night, there was always a fire, and Ugo was racing to the location to put it out. It drove them all crazy, including Gianni, but he never did anything to restrain Ugo. He always gave him free rein.

When they were at family parties, attended by most of Gianni's sisters and their children, Ugo was always the center of attention because he was the only boy. But on one occasion Aunt Rosa took Assunta aside and said she thought the boy might be hyperactive. Gina overheard their conversation, which as usual was in Italian, and at first she was puzzled by the word "*iperattivo*" but then she understood it.

"He's much more active than the girls were at his age," Assunta admitted. "But that's just how he is, and I can't do anything about it."

"Yes, you can. You can take him to a doctor."

"I take him to a doctor regularly."

"I mean a doctor who treats this kind of problem."

"You think it's a problem?"

"I think it is."

Assunta sighed. "Well, Nonna says Gianni was like that when he was a little boy."

"He *was* like that, and he drove us crazy."

"But you survived it."

"We survived it. But I wish our parents had done something about the problem."

"I think he'll grow out of it."

But he didn't grow out of it. In fact, he got worse. As soon as he started kindergarten the teacher complained about him. She said he never stopped talking, he never gave the other children a chance to do anything, and he never let them have any of the toys, which he collected and kept for himself.

Assunta finally took him to a doctor, who agreed with Aunt Rosa's diagnosis that Ugo was hyperactive. His solution was to give Ugo a drug that would calm him down.

"What kind of drug?" Gianni wanted to know. They were in the kitchen, and Gina was helping her mother make pasta.

"I can't pronounce the name of it," Assunta said. "But it's a drug they use to treat hyperactive children. He says it's safe."

"They always say drugs are safe. But they have side effects."

"I know. And I'm against giving him a drug."

"I am too. It could affect his brain."

"So we're not going to do what the doctor advises."

"No, we're not," Gianni said definitely.

At the time Gina, like her Aunt Rosa, wished her parents had done something about the problem, but she was resigned to living with it. Leonora had her own diagnosis, which she shared with Gina in the privacy of their bedroom: Ugo was a spoiled brat, just like their father, who had been spoiled by his mother and his sisters. Leonora, who was only ten, vowed that if she ever had a baby boy she wouldn't spoil him.

About a year later Gina was with her mother, her sister, and her brother in a store at the Cross County Shopping Center when

Ugo demanded a toy that had caught his eye. The toy had an electrical component, so it was expensive. Their mother patiently explained to Ugo that she couldn't afford to buy the toy, and that he didn't need it. Ugo reacted by throwing a tantrum, lying down on his back and furiously kicking his feet on the floor and screaming as if he was being tortured. People stopped and stared, but their mother stood firm on not buying the toy, and when they got home Ugo reported this injustice to their father, who after a brief discussion with their mother took him back to the store and bought the toy for him

A few years later at a family party Ugo persuaded one of his cousins to inject hot sauce into the lasagna so they could watch the faces of people after they took a bite of it. When their father, who had tried to quench the fire in his mouth by drinking water, sternly asked who was responsible, the cousin owned up, though she added in her defense that it had been Ugo's idea, and that he had supplied the hot sauce. Instead of scolding Ugo, their father praised what he had done as a clever prank.

A year or so later Ugo, who was sitting in their father's lounge chair, stuck out his leg as Gina walked by and tripped her. She hit the floor hard, breaking her arm, and when their father asked her how it had happened, she told the truth: her brother had deliberately tripped her. Ugo denied it, claiming he wasn't even in the chair and blaming the fall on Gina's clumsiness. After hearing both sides, their father took Ugo's side and told Gina: *"Devi stare più attenta."*

The family was still short of money while Ugo was attending St. Frances de Chantal, and since his grades were below average, he didn't get a scholarship, so they had to pay the full tuition, though by the time he was in sixth grade they were helped by the contribution of Gina's salary.

"He's not worth it," Leonora told her in the privacy of their bedroom.

"I know he's not," Gina said. "But he's our brother."

"I think there's a limit to what we have to do for our family. And he's beyond that limit."

"But if I didn't contribute my salary, our parents would make more sacrifices to send him to St. Frances. Mama might go back to work, and in her condition, that would be hard on her." Though their mother was then in remission from cancer, she was taking medication that among other side effects depleted her energy.

"Then you're doing it for mama, not for him."

"I guess that's how I should think about it."

When the time came for Ugo to go to high school, the family had plenty of money, so they didn't need Gina's contribution to send him to Fordham Prep, which cost a lot more than Preston. And since his grades were still below average, he didn't get a scholarship, so they had to pay the full tuition.

He was in his freshman year at the Prep when their mother died. Though Ugo was physically present at the wake and the funeral, he showed no signs of grief, and he acted as if his mind was elsewhere. And after that he didn't engage with the family.

At school there were no more complaints about his behavior, but there was no praise for his work. At home he retreated to his room where he spent hours playing video games, which from what Gina had glimpsed of them were invariably violent. He had to be called to come to dinner, and when he joined them he gulped down his food without a word and left his empty plate on the table for Gina to clear.

When he had to write a paper for a course, he came to Gina with a pad on which he had scrawled a few illegible notes and asked her to type it. There really wasn't a paper to type, so Gina ended up writing the paper for him. She wrote all his papers, and he got A's on them, but since he did so poorly on tests, exams, and classroom discussions his grades were between C and B. As she watched him walk up to get his diploma at graduation Gina couldn't help feeling that she had earned it, but she couldn't exchange a look with Leonora, who had a good excuse for not attending—she had given birth to Darcy only a few weeks ago.

He was accepted into the computer engineering program at Manhattan College, probably because he had gone to a good prep school. When he had to write a paper for a course he still came to

Gina, and she wrote papers on subjects that she didn't understand. But she evidently learned enough to help him get through the program.

When he graduated from Manhattan he got a job with IBM in Yorktown Heights where the company did a lot of its research. He continued living at home, where Gina cooked for him and did his laundry—she stopped short of cleaning his room. By then she was earning enough from her job at the printing company to afford her own apartment, but she couldn't leave her father knowing that he would be helpless without her, and it didn't require much more work to take care of her brother as well.

For the next six years Ugo enjoyed life as a bachelor, though instead of spending his money on clothes, shows, and presents as his father had, he spent it on electronic gadgets. His treasure was a collection of personal computers at every stage of development that he probably could have sold to a museum. He also had a collection of video games, which occupied most of his free time. He did have a social life, but unlike his father he hung out with guys, especially with guys who had been his classmates at the Prep. They went to bars in Yonkers and in the river villages, all the way up to Tarrytown. Presumably they met girls in these bars, but Gina never saw any evidence of a girlfriend. When they got together Gina and Leonora speculated about their brother's sexual identity, and they concluded that he was neuter because he didn't seem to be interested sexually in either girls or boys.

Then things changed. It happened accidentally because Ugo didn't like the city and had a policy of never going there. In fact, he never even went to the store on East 53rd Street to help his father. While he was getting his degree in computer engineering his excuse was that he had to study, and after he started his job at IBM it was that he had to work. But that year, instead of going to the St. Patrick's Day parade in Yonkers, Ugo was dragged by his buddies to the parade in Manhattan, and at an Irish bar in the east Sixties he met Eileen, who had come to the city for the day with three girlfriends. One thing they had in common was that they didn't like the city, and as far as Gina knew, they never went back there. When they started dating Ugo picked Eileen up in the suburb of Bridgeport where she lived, and they went to places in Fairfield, Westport, and Norwalk that suited her more than anything in her home town. The previous year, she had completed her bachelor's in accounting from Fairfield University, so she knew where to hang out in the area.

Two years after meeting they were married at St. Andrew, the church in her neighborhood that her family attended. It was a big wedding, with eight bridesmaids, including Gina who was persuaded to serve in this role, and a country club reception. For Eileen's father, who worked in maintenance at St. Vincent's Medical Center, paying for the wedding must have required a major sacrifice, but Eileen was his only daughter so at least it was a onetime hit.

Eileen couldn't wait to get out of Bridgeport, and after two years of living in an apartment in Stamford she and Ugo bought a house in Sudbury, where the average price of a house was almost as high as it was in Greenwich. Ugo worked in the research department of IBM in Yorktown Heights and Eileen worked in the accounting department of GE in Stamford, so their commutes from Sudbury were about equal. But they had nowhere near enough money for a down payment on the house, and after his splurge for the wedding Eileen's father couldn't help them, which left Gianni no apparent choice but to draw on the last of his reserves and provide the money. He made them sign a promissory note that under an accompanying contract was payable over ten years but would be forgiven when they produced a son.

Since they were still relatively young, they waited three years before they started trying to have a baby. Eileen announced their decision at a family party to celebrate the seventy-sixth birthday of Gianni, who frequently reminded them that he was running out of time. He was placated by the announcement, but as time passed with no results he was running out of patience.

"What's the problem?" he asked Eileen at the party for his seventy-eighth birthday.

"We don't know what the problem is," Eileen told him.

"Have you consulted a doctor?"

"Of course. He did a lot of tests on me, but he still doesn't know why I can't get pregnant."

"Maybe you need to change your technique."

Eileen blushed. "That's not the problem."

"Then what the hell is the problem?"

"We don't know."

Leonora already had two children, who by then were fourteen and seventeen, but they didn't count because they were girls. Her father loved them and was even demonstrative with them, which he hadn't been with his own daughters, but they weren't what he wanted. What he wanted was a boy, a grandson to carry on the family name.

When Gina got home from Ridge Hill she found Ron and Emilio in the kitchen with Colman. They were sitting at the table looking as if they had nothing urgent on their minds, but she had learned not to underestimate them. However they looked, their minds were busy working on the investigation.

"Ron has some news," Colman said. "He waited here to tell you directly."

"What is it?" she asked Ron, who had an empty coffee mug on the table in front of him.

"Yesterday morning the girl was on a flight to Miami."

"Was she on a connecting flight from there?"

"She bought a one-way ticket to Miami with no connecting flight beyond there."

"Then she was going to Miami?"

"It looks that way," Ron said, turning the mug around by its handle. "But maybe it's supposed to look that way."

"What do you mean?"

"Whoever lured her might have told her to buy a one-way ticket to Miami to make it harder to track her to her real destination."

"Okay. So we don't know if she was planning to stay in Miami or go somewhere else."

"That's right. But at least we've narrowed the search area."

"The Miami police are looking for her," Emilio said.

"You haven't been able to track her computer?"

"As far as we can tell, she hasn't used it."

"She's gone three days without using her computer?" Gina said. "I don't believe it. There must be something wrong with your tracking system."

"We use the system that the federal government uses," Ron said mildly. "But you have a point. The system doesn't always get things right."

"From the list of her friends on Facebook," Emilio said, "we identified five people who live in the area served by the Miami airport. They'll be found and questioned."

"There must be something more we can do," Gina said.

"I can't think of anything else," Ron told her. "But at least we know she went to Miami, and if she leaves Miami we can track her from there."

"I assume you'll watch the flights that go to San Pedro Sula," Colman said. "If she leaves Miami, then that would be her most likely destination."

"We're watching the airlines that go there, but we didn't know she went to Miami until this morning, so she could have flown to San Pedro Sula today."

"When would you know if she flew there today?"

"We'd know by tomorrow morning."

"In the meantime," Emilio said, "the police are looking for her in Miami and questioning those five people who live in the area."

"So we have to wait until tomorrow morning," Gina said, still wishing there was something more they could do. "You know, there were times when I wanted to shake her for being on her computer, and now I want to shake her for not being on it."

"Whoever lured her might have told her not to use it," Ron said, rotating his coffee mug.

"Well, if that's why she isn't using it, then she doesn't want us to track her."

"She probably just wants space," Colman said, "so she can find what she's looking for."

"If she'd just asked us, we would have taken her to San Pedro Sula to look for her mother."

"There are times," Ron said, "when kids have to do things by themselves, and maybe this is one of those times."

"But what she's doing is dangerous."

"When you were a kid, you never did anything dangerous?"

Gina paused to think. "The only dangerous thing I remember doing is taking a subway home from work one night when I had to stay late. But I wasn't a kid then."

"How old were you?"

"I was nineteen."

"Well, this kid's eighteen."

"Yeah, I know. But she seems a lot younger than I was at the same age."

"She *is* a lot younger emotionally," Colman said. "She missed out on a lot of things that most kids experience by the time they're her age."

"That's all the more reason to worry about her," Gina said. "She has so little experience in the real world."

Ron said nothing, and Emilio looked as if he was afraid to imagine his kids in their late teens.

When the police left a few minutes later, Gina realized that having taken time off her job, she had nothing to do but wait for news about Marisol. And having no interests outside of her family, she had nothing to distract herself. She had to live moment to moment with the fact that her goddaughter was missing and was probably in danger.

Sitting at the kitchen table, Gina remembered that Marisol had her usual appointment with Susan, her therapist, at four that afternoon, which had to be canceled. The girl met with Susan weekly, and every other month Gina and Colman met with Susan to talk about how things were going. The last time they met there had been no major issues, other than their frustration in trying to get the girl away from her computer.

She called Susan, who answered after three rings, saying: "Gina?"

"Hi. I'm calling because Marisol won't be able to make her appointment today."

"Oh, that's too bad," Susan said, sounding disappointed. "Is she all right?"

"I don't know," Gina admitted. "I don't know where Marisol is. She's been missing since Thursday evening."

"What?" There was a long pause. "Since Marisol was my last appointment, I can leave my office right now and stop by your place on my way home so you can tell me about it. Okay?"

"Okay." She welcomed the thought of talking with Susan, who might be able to tell her something that would help them find Marisol. She gave Susan directions to her house from the Tuckahoe Road exit off the Saw Mill River Parkway, which Susan would normally take from her office in Hastings to her home in Bryn Mawr.

Twenty minutes later she greeted Susan at the front door and led her into the kitchen, where they were joined by Colman.

Susan was a compact woman in her early forties with curly dark hair and compassionate dark eyes. She had two children, both of them girls and both of them in college now majoring in subjects that would prepare them for professions, one in healthcare and the other in education.

"Would you like coffee?" Gina asked.

"No, thanks," Susan said. "I've had enough coffee for today."

At the kitchen table she told Susan what had happened from the time Marisol hadn't come home on Thursday evening to their recent meeting with the police.

"So you think she might have gone to find her birth mother," Susan said.

"We can't think of anything else. Did she say anything to you about it?" Gina assumed that in this situation the rule of confidentiality was suspended.

Susan shook her head. "No. She hasn't talked about her birth mother in a long time."

"Has she talked about people she met online?" Colman asked.

"No. She never talked about what she does online. It's her secret place."

"I guess all kids need a secret place," Gina said, remembering the world of romantic stories that she had escaped to as a teenager.

"The problem is," Colman said, "she spends most of her life in the virtual world."

"I know she does," Susan said. "And that's why I focused our conversations on the real world."

"We had no idea what she did online," Gina said. "I mean, we just learned from the police that she pretended to be a boy."

"I'm not surprised. As we've discussed, she has gender identity issues. So I can see her trying out being a boy in the virtual world, where she thinks it's safe."

"But it's not safe," Colman said.

"It's not safe," Susan agreed. "In some respects, it's even more dangerous than the real world."

"We think someone lured her," Gina said, "by claiming to know where her birth mother is and promising to lead her there."

"That makes sense. Of course it assumes that she revealed her history online. And from what my patients tell me, they reveal everything online."

"Where they think it's safe," Colman said.

"Well, let's see how this scenario plays out," Susan said. "She pretends to be a boy, she reveals that she was abandoned by her birth mother, and someone lures her, believing she's a boy. Did she pretend to be younger than she is?"

"We don't know," Gina said.

"I assume there wasn't a picture of her."

"No. Thank God. We were afraid there would be pictures."

"I understand," Susan said. "So the guy who lured her doesn't know how old she is, but from the way she acts he guesses she's eleven or twelve."

In their conversations Susan often reminded them that due to the lack of continuity the girl hadn't developed normally during her first seven years of life, so you could deduct those years from her physical age to estimate her psychological age.

"Are you suggesting," Gina asked, "that the guy who lured her is a pedophile?"

"He could be. Whatever he is," Susan added, "he's not the kind of guy you want your goddaughter hanging out with."

"Why are you assuming it's a male?" Colman asked.

Susan turned and looked him directly in the eye. "Because more than ninety percent of the bad things that happen in this world are done by males."

"Okay," Colman said because he knew from experience that she was right. "But what do you think the guy will do when he finds out that she's a girl?"

"He'll be disappointed, to say the least. But he'll probably try to find some other use for her."

"You're not making me feel better," Gina said.

"I'm sorry," Susan said, "but I'm trying to understand what might have happened—and help you find her."

"The police haven't talked about the guy being a pedophile," Colman said. "So they should check that possibility in searching through the messages."

"You mean the messages on her Facebook?" Susan asked.

Gina nodded. "They have a list of all her friends, and they're analyzing the messages she exchanged with them."

"Have they found any messages about her birth mother?"

"No. The messages are about other things."

"As we told you," Colman said, "the police here tracked her to Miami, and the police there are questioning her Facebook friends who live in that area."

"If they aren't already doing it," Susan said, "they should check to see if any of those friends have a record of pedophilia."

"We'll suggest that," Gina said.

After a silence Susan said: "I should have probed more into what she was doing online. If I had, I might have seen this coming and prevented it."

Gina nodded. "Instead of trying to get her out of the virtual world, I should have gone into that world with her."

"She wouldn't have let you go there with her," Colman said. "It's her secret place."

"I guess she wouldn't have. I wouldn't have let my mother into my secret place."

"It's ironic," Susan said. "The corporations that hook the kids on social media know everything they're doing online, but their parents don't know anything."

"Well, kids should have some privacy," Colman said.

"They do have privacy—from their parents," Susan said. "But they don't have privacy from the malefactors who want to exploit them. That's the problem."

When Susan had left, Colman called Ron and suggested that they check to see if any of the girl's friends had a record of pedophilia. Ron said they had already done that, and so far they hadn't found any friend with such a record. But he said they would keep checking because his experience as a cop agreed with Susan's analysis as a therapist.

SIX

AT DINNER THAT evening Gina pursued a question that had arisen in their conversation with the police. They were at the kitchen table eating chicken, rice, and beans, which was one of Marisol's favorite dishes.

"You said that Marisol probably just wants space so that she can find what she's looking for," Gina said after swallowing. "But what is she looking for?"

"Ostensibly, her birth mother."

"You think it's something at a deeper level?"

"I think it is. I think she's looking for her identity."

"And she's hoping to find her identity with her birth mother?"

Colman nodded. "You know, I went to college with a guy who was adopted. He dropped out to look for his birth mother, hoping to find his identity."

"Did he find her?"

"No. Back then, they covered the tracks of birth mothers."

"Did he ever find his identity?"

"He eventually did, but he had to do it the hard way."

"You mean that if you're adopted, finding your birth mother is an easy way of finding your identity?"

"No. But it might seem like an easy way."

Gina reflected, eating a forkful of rice and beans. "I think it's been especially hard for Marisol to find her identity. As soon as Ugo and Eileen adopted her they changed her name, and maybe we added to the confusion by using her original name."

"But she wanted to keep her original name, and she wanted to keep her native language."

"Still, that put us at odds with her parents."

"We would have been at odds with them anyway. You've been at odds with your brother all your life."

"I know I have," Gina admitted. "We just don't have the same values, and I don't understand why. We were raised by the same parents."

"I think you take after your mother, and he takes after your father. But I didn't know them, so maybe I'm wrong."

"You're not wrong. But my father had some qualities that Ugo doesn't have. I mean, my father had a lot of energy. He worked hard, and he played hard. He did some stupid things, but he never stopped trying."

After a pause Colman said: "So you feel our being at odds with her parents contributed to Marisol's identity problem?"

"Well, I'm not sure I feel that way," Gina said, wondering. "I just feel we did something wrong."

"We probably did. But instead of trying to figure out what it was, we should try to figure out where she is, and we should find her. We should give our family another chance."

"My gut tells me she's on her way to San Pedro Sula, so I think we should go there."

"I checked the flights," Colman said. "We could leave at eight any morning and get there by one thirty in the afternoon."

"Then why don't we book a flight there?"

"I'm ready to go, but I think we should wait until the police confirm that she's gone there. If she's still in Miami, it won't help if we're in San Pedro Sula."

"I know. Well, Ron said that if she flew there yesterday, we'd know by tomorrow morning, right?"

"Right. So let's wait to hear from him before we do anything."

They were lingering at the table when her phone rang. It was within reach in case Marisol called or texted, and checking it she saw that the call was from Eileen. Not wanting to miss any piece of information, she answered the phone.

"I hope I'm not interrupting your dinner," Eileen said.

"No, we've finished eating."

"I called to ask you a favor." Eileen paused. "We have a mortgage payment at the beginning of next month, and since Ugo lost his job we don't have the money to pay it."

Gina listened, wondering if the favor was a loan to help them pay their mortgage.

"If he could get a consulting project, it would tide us over until he finds another job. So could you see if there's anything at your company?"

"Sure. But we do our computer work in Seattle."

"That's not a problem. Ugo could work remotely."

"What about GE? It's a big company."

"I asked them, and they said there isn't anything now."

"Well, couldn't you make the mortgage payment with your credit card?"

"No. We're maxed out on our credit card, and we can't pay off the balance by refinancing our mortgage like we did before."

"You refinanced your mortgage to pay off the balance of your credit card?"

"Several times. The rates on the mortgage were going down, so even though we ended up with more debt, our monthly payment wasn't much higher."

"If you don't mind my asking," Gina said, "how much is your monthly payment?"

"It's three thousand eight hundred dollars."

"Is that what it was when you bought the house?"

"It was around three thousand then."

"And you could afford that?"

"We almost could. Your father helped us make the payments at the beginning."

Her father had no money at that time, so Gina knew where the money came from to help them make the payments. "How much is your mortgage?"

"About nine hundred thousand dollars."

"How much is the house worth?"

"Not much more," Eileen said. "That's why we can't refinance the mortgage."

Gina didn't have the heart to ask where the money had gone.

From what she had observed on visits to Sudbury, it had gone to build a collection of electronic gadgets and to decorate the house in a style that would impress the neighbors, not to mention the gas-guzzling truck for Ugo and the high-end clothes for Eileen. "Okay, I'll see if we have a consulting project. But even if we do, it won't solve your problem, so Ugo better get off his ass."

Eileen sighed loudly enough to be heard over the phone. "That's what I told him, but he acts like he expects someone to call out of nowhere and offer him a job. And that doesn't happen in this economy."

"No. It doesn't." Feeling there wasn't much more she could say about her brother, Gina wondered if Eileen would ask about Marisol. She waited, giving Eileen a chance, but Eileen didn't ask about Marisol, and Gina didn't see any point in reminding Eileen that her daughter was missing, so she ended the call without mentioning it.

"What was that about?" Colman asked.

"They don't have money to pay their mortgage, so Eileen asked me to see if there's a consulting job at my company."

"You mean for Ugo."

"Yeah, for Ugo. It's always for Ugo," she said. "As far back as I can remember, it was always for Ugo. So am I a bad person for resenting that?"

"No. You're only human."

"She didn't ask about Marisol."

"I'm not surprised. When she said they were done with her, she meant it."

"So we're the only family that Marisol has. And if we fuck up—"

"We're not going to fuck up," Colman assured her. "We're going to find her, and we're going to bring her home."

Gianni's store continued to be successful through the 1980s, but after his son graduated from college he began to talk about selling the business. His goal was to get a million dollars for it, which he figured was enough to fund a good pension. He hired an agent to identify prospective buyers, and he talked with several people who were interested in buying the business, but none of them was willing to pay his price. Finally, he struck a deal with two men from Venezuela who had capital to invest in America, except that they needed time to get the money out of their country. The price was $1.1 million dollars, with $100,000 upfront in cash and the rest in notes payable over five years. This payment arrangement offered tax advantages for Gianni as well as a stream of income not only from the principal but also from the interest on the notes at the rate of ten percent.

Two weeks after he closed the deal he was off to Italy, leaving Gina responsible for the house and for Ugo, who commuted to his job at IBM in the Corvette Stingray that his father had given him as a graduation present. During the week Gina prepared dinner for him, which he usually ate in his bedroom while playing video games, but during the weekends he was on his own, sleeping all day and going out with his buddies at night, so she had time for a social life. She usually spent one of her free nights with Leonora and the other with a friend from Preston who like her was still single. They were both thirty-three, and they both believed they still had time to find the right man, get married, and have children. But in the meantime they were successful professionally.

Gina had been promoted several times, and now she was production manager for the Midwest region, where many of the independent presses that supplied the company were located. The three people who worked for Gina, two men and a woman, were responsible for matching the specifications of the projects with the capabilities of the presses. The projects included books, magazines, catalogs, reports, promotional materials for direct marketing, business forms, labels, and packaging. The four key criteria of any project were price, quality, timeliness, and reliability. Besides reviewing all the projects in her region, Gina also evaluated the capabilities of the presses, which required frequent trips to the Midwest.

On one particular trip during the time when her father was in Italy she was teamed with a regional sales manager so that he could acquire knowledge of the presses for responding to the needs of customers. There had been a few recent incidents in which the sales people had promised things that couldn't be delivered or at least not cost-effectively, so the purpose of the trip was to develop closer cooperation between sales and production.

The sales manager had joined the company in Europe and been transferred to the head office to gain experience in America. He was Danish, and his name was Christiaan. He was thirty-five, married with two young children, and he lived in Scarborough, which was on the same railroad line that Gina took from Yonkers to get into the city.

From the moment she had met him several months ago she had been attracted to him, and the more she worked with him, the more she liked him. But she didn't spend much time with him until that trip when they were on an airplane together for about two and a half hours flying to Chicago, and in a car for about an hour and a half driving to Milwaukee, which would be their base for visiting presses. What struck her was his desire to get to know her as a person, as evidenced by the questions he asked about her family, about her relationships with her parents and her siblings, and about her opinions on major issues in the world. It made her feel that she was worth getting to know, and that she was more than just a colleague to him.

As the trip progressed she learned more about him, and she found out that the happy-looking woman in the photo on his desk was suffering from severe depression and last winter had attempted suicide. He had only been able to take this trip and leave her for a few days because her sister had come from Denmark to be with her.

Gina felt a deep sympathy for him as well as admiration for him because she knew without his saying it that he would never leave his wife in her troubled state, and those feelings made her believe she was in love with him. By the end of the trip she believed he was also in love with her, but though they were in adjoining rooms at the hotel they resisted the temptation to go beyond a goodnight kiss.

They never took another trip together because in the fall the company transferred Christiaan back to Denmark, at his request, so that his wife could have special treatment there. But they kept in touch through occasional letters, in which they reported developments with their families.

In one such letter she told him about her father's return from Italy after more than a year, and about how the men who had bought his business defaulted on the first annual payment of the note. In subsequent letters she related how her father had taken legal action to repossess the business, only to find that there wasn't much left of it. The men had sold the inventory without replacing it, pocketed the cash, and then as soon as they realized that the game was over they returned to Venezuela.

"The whole thing was a scam," her father moaned, sitting at the kitchen table with a bottle of black Sambuca.

"You had an agent," Gina said. "Wasn't he supposed to check on those guys?"

"I didn't use him. I did the deal directly so I wouldn't have to pay a commission."

"But you must have checked on them."

"I did. I got a bank reference on them, and it was positive."

"And you never had an inkling that it was a scam?"

"I never did," her father said mournfully. "I trusted them. They were *paesani*."

Gianni had spent most of the upfront cash from the deal, and since he had drawn a minimal salary from the business, extracting cash in other ways, he received only about half of the social security that he might have been entitled to. At the same time he was personally liable for the store's lease, having sublet the space to the men from Venezuela, and the lease had eleven years left on it. He had no savings because he had counted on the sale of the business to fund his retirement, so he was in a precarious financial situation.

His solution was to revive the store, and he turned to Gina to help him. At first he only asked her to go to the store and help him do the inventory, which she gladly did. They worked all day and found that he would need about thirty thousand dollars to rebuild the inventory to a level where the store would be viable. Gianni had only about half of that amount, and he asked Gina if she could provide the other half. She had that amount in savings, which she had accumulated after she stopped having to contribute her salary to the family. In return for her financial support her father offered to make her half owner of the business. She didn't want to own half of the business, she wanted to pursue her career, but she didn't see any choice but to lend her father the money to rebuild the inventory, and when she refused to accept half of the business he was offended and took it personally, so she finally agreed to accept his offer, though she realized that she could be trapped by her stake in the business.

Within a year the store recovered, and over the next several years it not only provided a living for her father, it also gave him something to do. But in addition to helping him with the business, he expected Gina to run the big house and take care of him. And Ugo, who at that time still lived at home, expected Gina to take care of him. She had less patience with Ugo than she had with her father, who was getting old and slowing down, and there were times when she had more than enough of Ugo.

One time he barged into her bedroom at three in the morning and woke her up, saying: "There's no milk."

"Milk?" She had to clear her brain before she knew what he was talking about. Every day he drank a quart of milk and ate a bag of cookies, usually in the wee hours of the morning during a break from his video games.

"You didn't buy enough milk. We're out of it."

"How old are you?" she asked after rubbing her eyes.

"I'm thirty. What's that got to do with it?"

"Milk is for babies, not for people your age."

"Don't give me that shit. You're just trying to cover up your failure."

"My failure? To do what?"

"To buy enough milk."

"Look, you're the only person in this house who drinks milk, and if you want milk you can buy it yourself. It's not my job to take care of babies."

"I'm going to tell papa," he whined.

"Go and tell him. Wake him up and see how he reacts."

It didn't get better. But a year later he met Eileen, and two years later he married her and finally moved out of the house. By then her father was no longer paying close attention to the business. Instead, he was spending more and more time at the senior center in Throgs Neck, where he went almost every day after driving to Manhattan in the morning to check the store. He had hired a man in his forties named Richard who was responsible for the daily operations of the store. While Gina had some doubts about him, she wasn't about to give up her career and take over the store as long as it was surviving.

One night her father insisted that she watch a video of him performing at the senior center. He strolled the floor with a wireless microphone, pretending he was Frank Sinatra, and singing the familiar songs: "My Way," "New York, New York," "Three Coins in a Fountain," "The Lady is a Tramp," "One for My Baby," and "Strangers in the Night."

When the tape was finally done, her father asked her: "What do you think?"

"You have a good voice, and you perform those songs well."

"Yeah, but?" There was a long pause.

"You're not Frank Sinatra."

"I know I'm not Frank Sinatra," he bellowed. "But I could have been a star in my own right."

"Maybe you could have been. I don't know. Why is it so important to you?"

"Because—" He stopped, at a loss for words. "Because it makes me feel special."

"You're special, papa. You don't have to prove it. But if you enjoy performing, then do it for the fun of it."

"You mean you don't take it seriously?"

"I take everything about you seriously. I'm only suggesting that *you* don't take it seriously. If you don't, you'll have more fun at it."

Not long after this conversation her father came to her with the proposal to lend Ugo money for the down payment on the house in Sudbury. She asked him where the money would come from, and he said he could borrow it from a bank by pledging the assets of the business. She reminded him that she was half owner of the business, and he said he knew, which was why he was asking her permission to borrow the money. Not seeing any choice, she agreed to the proposal, but when the bank drew up the documents for the loan she saw that they wanted personal guarantees from her father and her as owners of the business.

"I won't do it," she told him as she drove him home from the meeting with the bank. "I've done enough for Ugo. I paid for St. Frances, I wrote all his papers, and I've been taking care of him since mama died. If they want to buy a house in a place like Sudbury, they should save the money to pay for it. They both have good jobs."

"But they want to have a family, so they need a house."

"They can buy a house in Yonkers."

"She's from Connecticut."

"Then they can buy a house in Bridgeport. That's where she grew up."

"She wants to live in a better area, which I can understand."

"She doesn't have to buy a house in Sudbury to live in a better area. I'm sure there are other good areas in Connecticut that aren't as expensive as Sudbury."

"Well, that's what she wants, and Ugo only wants to do what his wife wants."

"Since when did Ugo ever want to do anything that someone else wanted? If you ask me, Ugo wants to live in an upscale area as much as she does."

"Maybe he does. But I want my grandson to grow up in a better area than I did."

"What's wrong with Throgs Neck?"

"It has too many Puerto Ricans."

"Well, if it's so bad, then why do you go back there almost every day?"

"I go back to our senior center. We're mostly *paesani*. But we're all getting older, and soon there won't be any of us left."

She was touched by this statement despite the racism that preceded it, and she realized how important it was to her father to impress the members of his community as long as there were any of them left.

"If you sign the guarantee," he finally said, "I'll give you full ownership of the business."

"I don't want full ownership of the business. I want to pursue my career."

"But you could be your own boss."

"I have a good boss. I don't need to be in charge."

"Well, I need you to be in charge. Richard's not working out, and if someone more competent doesn't manage the business, it won't survive."

"So you want me to manage the business?"

"You're the only one of my kids who has any business sense."

"And what if I won't do it?" she asked, pushing back.

"The business won't survive," her father said. "I'm too old to save it by myself."

"I won't do it," she wanted to tell him. But she knew she wouldn't be doing it for her brother, she would be doing it for her father, and if the business didn't survive she would end up supporting him anyway.

For five years she ran the business, and she made enough money to support her father and herself and to pay back the bank loan. But it was getting harder to survive as an independent store selling high-end kitchen equipment. A national chain opened a store in the city only a few blocks away, and then another chain entered the market. The chains had the advantage of buying in a huge volume and having significantly lower costs, and it was only a matter of time before they put independent stores out of business.

Gina kept the store running until six months after her father died, when the lease was up for renewal. The landlord wanted three times as much rent, and by then the business had trouble paying the current rent, so she had a liquidation sale, and she closed the store.

At that point she had no career and no income, but she got a job in the kitchen department of Macy's at the Cross County Center. She had just turned forty-five.

Since she didn't have enough income to pay the taxes and other expenses of the big house, she put it up for sale. The housing market was buoyant then, and she had no trouble selling the house. The proceeds went into her father's estate, to be divided equally among his three children. As executrix of the estate she had to deal with the notes that Ugo had signed when he borrowed money to buy the house in Sudbury. Of course he hadn't paid anything back, and for a while Gina considered deducting the amount of the loan from Ugo's share of the estate, which would have been fair, but she relented, recognizing that her action might have been tainted by her negative feelings toward Ugo. So after getting approval from Leonora, who would have benefitted by the reduction of Ugo's share, she tore up the notes and burned them.

"But that's it," Leonora told her. "I'm not doing anything more for him."

Gina felt the same way, but she couldn't be sure that in the future she wouldn't have to do something more for her brother.

The closing on the sale of her father's house and the liquidation of his business were handled by Colman, who was recommended by a friend in Yonkers. The friend had built up Colman so much that Gina expected to be disappointed when she met him, but she immediately recognized his good qualities, and she was attracted to him in much the same way that she had been attracted to Christiaan. After hearing about him Leonora suggested that Gina was attracted to Colman because he was a good man, just as she was attracted to Jerry because he was a good man. And maybe that was it. In any case they started seeing each other, and by their third date she had heard his story.

Colman had grown up in the Bronx, and not having money to pay for college, he joined the marines and did a tour of duty in

Vietnam. Upon his discharge he applied to Fordham University, was accepted, and completed a degree in business administration. At that point, instead of taking a job with a company, he joined the Peace Corps and was sent to Chile with the mission of helping small businesses with finance and accounting. He spent almost three years there, serving in Talcahuano and Concepción. In the latter city he met a young woman, a high school teacher, whose name was Lucía. They fell in love, and for a while they were happy together, working in their professions and seeing each other. But then a friend of Lucía's was arrested by the government and made to disappear. It was less than three years since the democratically elected government of Salvador Allende was overthrown by the military, with General Augusto Pinochet assuming control as dictator, and there were still pockets of resistance, especially among young people. Lucía, who was never a supporter of the military government, was radicalized by the disappearance of her friend, and she became an activist. Colman joined her, and they participated in protests against the military. At one of these protests they were both arrested. They were separated, and Colman spent eleven weeks in prison not knowing what had happened to Lucía, only to learn on his release that she had been made to disappear. The standard procedure was to torture people, kill them, and dispose of their remains where they could never be found. The official who released Colman told him that he was being given special treatment because his country was a strong ally of Pinochet, but that he would have to leave Chile immediately, on a flight they had arranged for him.

Under duress he returned to New York, where he was torn between taking up arms against his own government and falling into a dark pit. Eventually he pulled himself together and went to law school at Fordham and earned his degree. For a while he worked at a law firm in White Plains, where he was periodically assigned to defendants in criminal cases who couldn't afford to pay for a lawyer. Meanwhile, he pursued a course of legal action against Pinochet for crimes against humanity. It got nowhere, and he decided that he could make better use of his time helping immigrants in Yonkers. So he moved to Nodine Hill and set up an office in his house from which he could serve the community.

Gina was moved by his story, and her love for him was deepened by her sympathy and admiration for him. Two years later they were married at the church of Our Lady of Mt. Carmel with only their immediate families attending. Gina was forty-seven, and Colman was fifty-one.

Later that evening Ron and Emilio dropped by the house to tell them the latest development. They were still cleaning up after dinner, so they all sat down at the kitchen table.

Gina got coffee and set out on a plate about a dozen of the biscotti she had made on Wednesday evening with Marisol, which they did whenever they had a craving for these hard cookies with almonds in them. They were so much better than the ones you could buy in stores that Marisol would eat them only if they were made in their own kitchen.

"Our geek found something that could be helpful," Ron said, taking a cookie. "The girl exchanged messages with a guy who lives in Miami. I'll let Emilio tell you about it because the messages were all in Spanish."

"The guy lives in South Beach," Emilio said. "It's a hip area. It's the closest thing they have to Greenwich Village."

"What my partner's trying to say," Ron said, "is that it has a gay community."

"So what does that have to do with anything?" Gina asked.

"Remember," Emilio said, "your goddaughter pretended to be a boy, and she might have come across as being gay."

"I can see that," Colman said.

"The question never came up in their exchange of messages, but it was lying there below the surface. I mean, the guy kept talking about the arty people he could introduce her to."

"But she's not interested in arty people," Gina said.

"Maybe she's not," Emilio said. "But she pretended to be interested in them. She went along with the whole scenario."

"How far did she go?" Colman asked.

"She went as far as telling the guy she planned to go to South Beach so she could meet these people."

"That doesn't sound like her," Gina said, shaking her head.

"I know it doesn't," Ron said. "But you never know what people will do when they go online. I mean, what about that Congressman who texted pictures of himself in his underwear? I'm sure his mother would say it didn't sound like him."

"Suppose she went to South Beach," Colman said, "and the guy found out that she's a girl. How do you think he would have reacted?"

"He would have been pissed," Emilio said. "But I don't think he would have hurt her. He didn't sound like a violent guy."

"I can understand the attraction," Gina said, "if she thought she was going to meet people who could be her friends, but would that have been strong enough to lure her?"

"Maybe," Ron said. "You never know what could lure a kid."

"The Miami police are questioning him," Emilio said. "We should hear from them soon."

"Okay," Colman said. "Do you have any more leads from her Facebook?"

"We have a few," Ron said, taking another cookie from the plate, "but this is the one with the most activity. And so far it's the only one in Miami."

"We could be missing some activity," Emilio said, "because the girl might not have used Facebook to communicate with all of them. She might have used email with some of them, and we don't have access to her email."

"The kids don't use email," Colman pointed out. "They use text messages."

"Well, we don't have access to her text messages either."

After a silence Gina asked: "So you haven't found anyone on her Facebook who lives in San Pedro Sula?"

"No, we haven't," Ron said.

"What about Tegucigalpa?" Colman asked.

"We haven't found anyone who lives in Honduras."

"The trail still leads to Miami," Emilio said, "so we're focusing on that city."

"You know," Ron said, contentedly munching, "these are the best damn biscotti I ever had. They're even better than the ones my mother made."

"Thank you," Gina said. "When you find Marisol, I'll make a batch especially for you."

After the police had left, Gina and Colman went into the living room and sat down on the sofa where Marisol had sat with them so many times to watch a movie or a baseball game. As if she was there, they allowed enough space for her between them.

"What do you think?" Colman asked her.

"I think," Gina said, "she could have been lured by the guy in South Beach. I mean, I'm willing to admit that I have no idea what she does online. And it wouldn't surprise me if she texted pictures of herself in her underwear."

"It would surprise me. I think she has more sense than that Congressman."

Gina laughed in relief. "But I still don't think the promise of friends would be enough to lure her. I think it had to be something more."

"So we're back on the trail to San Pedro Sula?"

"I think we are. Ron said we'd know by tomorrow morning if she was on a flight there."

"If you want," Colman told her, "we can go to my office now and book flights for the day after tomorrow."

"Then let's book them. At least it would make me feel like we're doing something."

"We can always cancel the tickets if we don't need them."

"I hope we don't need them," Gina said. "I hope they find her in South Beach. But I just have a feeling they won't."

She followed him into his office, where he sat down at his desk and activated his computer. She stood and waited while he booked the flights. She remembered what Emilio had said about San Pedro Sula: it had the highest murder rate of any city in the world. It didn't bother her that she might have to go there, but it worried her that Marisol might have gone there.

"It's done," Colman said, rising from his chair.

She met him in a close hug that while it lasted made her feel better. And then she had to face another night of lying awake and imagining the worst.

Gina spent the rest of the evening in Marisol's room dealing with the mess. She picked up things and put them away. She sorted through the clothes on the floor, she washed them, dried them, folded them, and put them in drawers or hung them in the closet. It was as if she believed that putting the room in order would help to bring her goddaughter home.

SEVEN

THE NEXT DAY, which was Sunday, they went to the early mass at Our Lady of Mt. Carmel, and they prayed for Marisol's safe return. The last time Gina had prayed for anything so urgently was when her mother was diagnosed with cancer. It would have taken a miracle to cure her mother, whereas in this situation Gina had more hope, and she had more confidence in the people who were helping her, but she still felt the need for divine intervention.

When they got home they had ciabatta rolls and coffee at the kitchen table. They were still at the table when Ron called and told them that Marisol had been on a flight from Miami to San Pedro Sula the previous day. Emilio had contacted the police in San Pedro and given them a photo of Marisol as well as the address of the orphanage in case she decided to go there. The guy in Miami who had exchanged Facebook messages with Marisol turned out to be a false lead because when he was questioned he still thought Marisol was a boy.

After ending the call Colman tried to get them on a flight to San Pedro that day, but there were no direct flights from New York, there was only one flight a day from Miami, and there was no way they could make that flight because it left at twelve fifty, and it would take three hours to fly to Miami, not including the time to get to the airport, check in, and go through security. So they had to resign themselves to going on the flight they had booked for the next day, which meant that Marisol would be in San Pedro two days ahead of them.

Having to wait almost a full day before she could do anything, Gina called Leonora and arranged to have brunch with her. At least that would kill some time, and she needed to bring her sister up to date. She had been waiting until they had more information

96

before upsetting Leonora with the news that Marisol was missing. Leonora really cared about the girl, and she had always been on hand to help with her.

Leonora still lived in Bryn Mawr, in the house that she and Jerry had bought more than thirty years ago—without any help from her father. Her husband was now a manager of the bus company, and their two girls were grown up. The older one, Darcy, was thirty-two and worked as a teacher at a middle school in Yonkers. She lived in the neighborhood of St. Brigid with her husband, a fireman, and their two girls. The younger one, Selma, was twenty-nine and worked as a paramedic for an emergency medical service in White Plains, where she lived in an apartment. According to her mother, she was having such a good time as a single woman that she wasn't even considering the possibility of marriage.

From the time her children were old enough to be in school, Leonora had held a variety of jobs, which included being a waitress and a bartender. Her present job was managing the office of a beer distributor on Saw Mill River Road. She had stayed in this job for more than five years, a record for her, and she wasn't looking around for another job.

They met at a Greek diner on Saw Mill River Road. Leonora got there first, and Gina found her sitting at a table in a booth with a glass of white wine in front of her. Leonora got up, and they hugged, and then they both sat down.

The waiter came right over and asked Gina if she would like something to drink. She told him she would have what her sister was having. As soon as he had brought the wine and left them, Leonora said: "You look worried. What's wrong?"

"It's Marisol," Gina said. "She went to Honduras to find her birth mother."

"I thought her birth mother was killed in a car accident."

"We thought so too, but it turns out that she was alive at the time of the adoption."

"You mean our dear brother and his wife lied to us?"

"I guess they were trying to prevent Marisol from trying to find her birth mother."

"You mean Meredith," Leonora said, imitating their brother.

"She's been missing since Thursday evening. She came home from school while I was at work and she packed some things and she just took off."

"Why didn't you tell me sooner?"

"I didn't want to worry you for no reason. I mean, we thought she might turn up, and then the police started looking for her. They tracked her to Miami, and they thought she planned to stay there, but yesterday they tracked her to Honduras."

"The Yonkers police were able to do that?"

"They're better than you think. In fact, they're really good."

Leonora took a sip of wine, and then she said: "So why did she suddenly want to find her birth mother?"

"We don't know. We think it could have something to do with finding her identity."

"I understand. But how would she know where to look for her birth mother?"

"We think she was lured by someone online who claimed to know where her birth mother was."

"So she revealed her history online?"

"We think she did. But we don't know what she did online."

"Well, I'm glad my girls didn't grow up with computers and smartphones. You should hear the problems that Darcy has with her students."

"Yeah, I can imagine," Gina said. "Anyway, we think she was lured by someone, and now she's in San Pedro Sula, which has the highest murder rate of any city in the world."

"They have a lot of drug activity."

"How do you know?"

"I saw a report on television about how drugs that used to come from Mexico are coming from Honduras."

"We assume the guy who lured her wants something from her."

"Oh, yeah. He probably wants money. How much money did she take with her?"

"Two thousand dollars. She bought a one-way ticket, which cost about four hundred dollars, so she still must have about sixteen hundred dollars."

"That's a lot of money for someone in Honduras. According to that report it's one of the poorest countries in the Western Hemisphere."

"But what if he wants something else?"

"What do you mean?" Leonora asked as if she could guess but didn't want to say it.

"What if he wants to sell her body?"

"It's possible. She's a pretty girl, and I assume she posted pictures of herself on Facebook."

"No, she didn't. She pretended to be a boy named Mario."

"A boy? Why would she do that?"

"I don't know. Maybe she was experimenting with gender identities."

"Selma did that. During one of her phases she hung out with boys and tried to be one of them. Of course it didn't work."

The waiter, who had been respecting their privacy, finally came over and took their food orders: eggs benedict for Leonora and a mushroom omelet for Gina.

"You said she bought a one-way ticket," Leonora said.

"She did, and that worries me too. It indicates that she was planning to stay there."

"You mean with her birth mother."

"Yeah, with her birth mother. And the last thing we know about this woman, she was a prostitute working on the street."

"How long ago was that?"

"About five years ago."

"Then she's probably not alive."

"I hope she's not," Gina said. "I mean, if she's not it would simplify things."

"It would stop Marisol from trying to find her, but it wouldn't solve the problem."

"You mean the problem of finding an identity. But there's no easy way. Remember what you had to go through."

"I remember. And I saw what my kids had to go through. So I agree, there's no easy way. And maybe Marisol will learn from this experience."

"Maybe she will. But I wish she'd gone somewhere else."

"I assume you're going there."

"We're leaving early tomorrow morning."

"I'll pray for her, and I'll pray for you. I'll even pray for Colman, though he doesn't need it."

That got a smile out of Gina, who reached across the table and took her sister's hand.

After trying for about five years to have a baby Eileen decided that it wasn't going to happen, so she began the process of adoption. Their first choice was to adopt a baby boy in America, but after encountering complications they widened their focus to include Europe, where in two situations their hopes were raised but the deals fell through. At that point, on the advice of the lawyer they had hired to help them, they shifted their focus to Latin America, where after six months the lawyer found a baby boy in Brazil that he said was from a good family, implying that it was white. But that deal also fell through, and after so much disappointment they accepted a girl in Honduras who had mocha skin and was almost seven. By then they were into the process so deeply that they were ready to settle for anything.

Of course a nonwhite girl from Honduras wasn't at all what Gianni wanted, and within a few months of seeing the child he died—according to his last words—of a broken heart. Since an adopted girl didn't meet the terms of the loan he had made to Ugo and Eileen, the promissory note wasn't forgiven, and it went into the estate, along with other unpaid notes.

Though the lawyer who had handled the adoption insisted that the girl had already been baptized, Ugo and Eileen no longer trusted him, so they arranged for the sacrament to be performed at the local church. They asked Gina to be the godmother, a role for which she had experience because she was the godmother of Leonora's two children. A colleague at work jokingly remarked that it sounded like she was becoming a professional godmother, which made Gina wonder if that would be her role in life.

They hadn't told her about the name change, and the first time she heard "Meredith" was when the priest used it in the ceremony. Standing at the baptismal font, she wasn't in a position to question the name, but later she demanded an explanation.

"Why did you change her name?" she asked Ugo as soon as the girl had gone downstairs to watch television. They were sitting at the counter in the kitchen while Eileen opened a cheese dip she had bought at the supermarket.

"No one can pronounce her previous name," Ugo said, making one of his usual categorical statements.

"She can pronounce it," Gina said. "And so can a lot of other people. But she can't pronounce the name you gave her."

"Meredith? Anyone can pronounce that."

"We wanted her to have an American name," Eileen said, bringing the dip and some crackers to the counter.

"So you think that if her name is Meredith, no one will notice that she's Latina?"

"They'll be more likely to treat her like an American," Ugo said.

"Then why don't you change your name to Hugh?"

"It's too late now. People already know me by Ugo." He took a swig of beer from a can of Bud Light. "But I wish our parents hadn't given us Italian names."

"You could have changed your name."

"I know. But by the time I was old enough, it was too late."

"Well, I don't think you had a right to change her name."

"What do you mean I don't have a right?" Ugo said indignantly. "I adopted her. I saved her from dying on the streets of that godforsaken city."

"Whatever you saved her from, you should respect what she was, and the name she had for the first seven years of her life was part of her identity."

"We want her to forget what she was," Eileen said, spreading cheese dip thickly on a cracker. "We want her to become a normal American girl."

"Did you explain that to her?"

"We can't explain anything to her," Ugo said. "She doesn't understand a single word of English, and we sure as hell don't know Spanish."

"If you were going to adopt a child from Latin America, why didn't you learn some Spanish?"

"We didn't think it was necessary," Eileen said, "because we were expecting to get a baby."

"Well, maybe you should learn some Spanish now."

"We don't need to learn Spanish," Ugo said. "The girl needs to learn English."

Marisol did learn English. Within about six months she was speaking English fluently. But she maintained her native language, which wasn't easy in an area where Spanish was spoken only by people who did construction and mowed lawns and cleaned houses and worked in restaurants. She watched Spanish television, she read Spanish books, and she talked with the "illegals" as Ugo called the women who relieved his wife of the drudgery of cleaning her house. Refusing to accept this emblem of the girl's identity, Ugo and Eileen complained that she was just like all those people who came here speaking Spanish and wouldn't give it up. Ironically, Ugo had grown up in a house with grandparents who spoke only Italian and parents who spoke Italian at home, but for some reason—maybe because he was seven years younger, or because he desperately wanted to be a real American, unlike his grandparents and his parents and his siblings—he had never learned a word of Italian.

Gina met Colman less than a year after the arrival of Marisol, and the first time she took him to Sudbury to meet her brother and sister-in-law there was an argument. From the years he had spent in Latin America and then in a neighborhood where the main language was Spanish, he was perfectly fluent in the language. In fact, native speakers of Spanish had told Gina that he didn't have a trace of a gringo accent. So when he was introduced to the girl, Colman spoke Spanish with her as if he knew instinctively that she preferred to speak in her native language. And she responded to Colman as if he was the father she dreamed of having, which sparked a flame of jealousy in Ugo.

When the girl had gone downstairs to watch television he bluntly told Colman: "We don't want her to speak Spanish. We want her to learn English."

"Since she lives in a house where she only hears English," Colman said, "she won't have any trouble learning it."

"We want her to give up Spanish," Eileen said.

"Why?" Colman asked.

"So she can fit in with our community."

"You mean she won't fit in with your community if she knows another language?"

"People here speak English," Ugo said, "and if they hear her speaking Spanish, they're going to wonder about her."

"What are they going to wonder?"

"They're going to wonder if she belongs here."

"You mean they might think her mother cleans houses?"

"They might," Ugo said.

"So it's about you," Colman said. "It's not about her."

"She's our adopted daughter," Eileen said. "Whatever she says or does reflects on us."

"Well, I guess that explains why you changed her name to Meredith."

"You told him?" Ugo said to Gina.

"Of course I told him. I wanted him to know what he was getting into when I brought him here to meet you."

"You changed her name," Colman said, "so people won't think she's Latina."

"That's right," Ugo said. "We don't want our daughter to be mistaken for one of those people who don't belong in America."

"But you must be aware of the fact that not too long ago a person named Ugo Moretti would have been regarded as one of those people who don't belong in America, as would a person named Colman Hayes."

"That's ancient history. It has nothing at all to do with the present."

"It's only two generations ago. And I should point out that there are people who came to this country speaking only Spanish whose grandchildren speak only English."

"That proves our point. We want her to speak only English."

"But she's not the grandchild of people who came here two generations ago. She came her less than a year ago."

"You're not her father," Ugo said, "so you have no right to interfere with what we're trying to do for her."

"I don't have a right to interfere, but I do have a right to comment," Colman said quietly, "because I'm going to become a member of this family."

"You didn't tell us," Eileen said, turning to Gina.

"We came here to tell you," Gina said. "But Ugo got into an argument about Marisol—"

"Her name is Meredith," Ugo said.

"She introduced herself to me as Marisol," Colman said.

"I didn't hear that. What did she say?"

"She said: *'Me llamo Marisol. Es un gran placer conocerle.'*"

"She should have introduced herself in English."

"I invited her to speak to me in Spanish."

"Well, you shouldn't have," Ugo said curtly. "And don't you ever do it again."

As if she hadn't heard this exchange, Eileen said: "So tell us what's happening with you guys."

"We're getting married," Gina said.

"That's wonderful. When is the wedding?"

"Whenever the priest has time to do it."

"Then you're not going to have a big wedding," Eileen said, sounding disappointed.

"No, we're only going to have the immediate family."

While Eileen prepared dinner Gina gave her more details about the wedding, and she overheard the men talking about baseball, a safe subject. Still, there was an edge in Ugo's voice that indicated how he felt about Colman. She hadn't expected them to be buddies, but she had hoped they would get off to a better start.

The dinner was ready-made lasagna that Eileen had bought at Stew Leonard's, accompanied by a salad of prewashed lettuce that came with plastic packets of premixed Caesar dressing, preground Parmesan cheese, and prefabricated croutons. The lasagna was heated in the microwave oven and the salad was tossed in a plastic bowl. When everything was ready Ugo yelled down the basement stairs: "Meredith! Come up for dinner."

A few months later Gina and Colman were married at Our Lady of Mt. Carmel. Leonora and Jerry were the witnesses. Ugo and Eileen attended, but they didn't bring Marisol. They all had dinner at Tres Chaves, a Portuguese restaurant on Myrtle Street, up the hill from Nepperhan Avenue. As usual, Ugo ordered the most expensive item on the menu.

It took Gina only a week to move out of her apartment on North Broadway and into Colman's house on Linden Street. She had just gotten settled when Eileen called and asked if Meredith could spend the weekend with her. Eileen explained that they needed a break from the girl, who was giving them a lot of trouble.

On Friday afternoon Gina and Colman met Eileen at exit 27 of the Merritt Parkway, just over the border in Connecticut. They got out of the car and waited for Marisol to emerge from the sport utility vehicle that seemed to be standard equipment for people who lived in the suburbs. The girl carried a tote bag with things she needed for the weekend, and she stood there looking out of context. Responding to her need, Gina hugged her. She noticed that Marisol didn't quite meet her in the hug, as if she didn't feel worthy of being hugged.

Then Colman gave her an abrazo, saying: "*Estamos muy contentos de que pases el fin de semana con nosotros.*"

"*Yo también estoy contenta,*" Marisol responded.

On the trip back to Yonkers they spoke Spanish, which seemed to establish a comfort zone for Marisol, and except for a few lapses when Gina had to resort to English they continued speaking Spanish through the weekend.

That began a pattern of Marisol spending weekends with them once or twice a month. She played with kids in the neighborhood who spoke Spanish, and she went with Gina and Colman to the mass in Spanish at Our Lady of Mt. Carmel. Gina had stopped going to church after the death of her father, who had made her go to church every Sunday in the old neighborhood, but she was conscientious about her duty to raise her goddaughter in the Catholic faith, which evidently Ugo and Eileen weren't doing. The mass in Spanish brought back memories of going to the mass in Italian with her grandparents and parents, and it helped Gina improve her Spanish.

On Fridays they ate fresh flounder from the seafood market at Getty Square accompanied by cheese ravioli, which Gina made from scratch, and on Saturdays they went to Caridad, a Dominican restaurant on South Broadway, where Marisol especially liked the roast pork with rice and beans. She also liked being able to speak Spanish with the waiters, who were Mexican. They treated her as if she was a member of their family.

When Marisol visited them she always brought the Apple computer that Ugo had bought for her seventh birthday. He claimed that it would help her develop valuable skills, but Gina suspected that its real purpose was to occupy the girl so she wouldn't need so much attention. It wasn't long before she was addicted to her computer, relying on it for stimulation. And it became an issue when during a visit Marisol brought it to the dinner table.

"We have a rule," Colman told her, speaking in Spanish. "We don't allow computers when we're together as a family."

"My parents let me bring it to the table."

"We don't care what your parents let you do. In our house you obey our rules."

"Then maybe I don't want to come to your house."

"That's your choice. We don't make you come here. But we love you, and we want you to come here."

Without a word the girl got up from the table and went upstairs, taking her computer.

They waited, hoping she would return, and after about ten anxious minutes she did return, and she went to Gina and hugged her and pressed her face against her, saying: "I'm sorry. I do want to come to your house."

"We want you to come here," Gina told her, rubbing her back. "We love you."

When Marisol spent the weekend with them they usually tried to do something that the girl couldn't do in Connecticut. They took her on a boat ride that circled the Statue of Liberty. They took her to the top of the Empire State Building, to Radio City, and to Times Square. They took her to "The Sound of Music," where she ended up sitting in Colman's lap so that she could see over the heads of the people in front of them, and she especially liked the scenes when the children were on stage. In the late summer they took her to the Dutchess County Fair, where she liked everything, beginning with the baby animals and ending with the scary rides. Gina had never liked those rides, so she watched while Marisol and Colman went up together in a machine that looked like a giant octopus, and she heard Marisol's shrieks of fear when they were turned upside down. Surprisingly, she wanted to do that ride again, but they redirected her attention to the games where you could win prizes by knocking over milk bottles with a baseball. Marisol hurled the ball as if she were trying to break the bottles, and she didn't hit a single bottle, but she had a good time trying, and she kept playing until she finally won a prize, a little pink bear. And sometimes they took her to a movie, though it wasn't easy to find one that was both suitable and interesting,

Whatever they did, they always had time for Colman and Marisol to play soccer in the backyard, which was just big enough for them to practice getting around each other with the ball and kicking it into a garbage can that lay on its side. Though Gina wasn't a sports fan, even she could tell that Marisol had a lot of talent, and she agreed with Colman that it would be good for her to play on a team, which would help her make friends.

They went to Sudbury about every three months, but not for the major holidays, which Ugo and Eileen celebrated with her family in Bridgeport. On those occasions Ugo was barely civil to Colman, and he made a point of mocking the girl's original name by yelling: "Mary Sue, come up for dinner. Mary Sue, bring me a beer."

On one of these visits Gina broached the subject of enabling Marisol to play soccer on a community team. They had finished dinner, but they were still sitting at the table, and Marisol was downstairs watching television.

"She can't play soccer," Ugo said.

"You mean she's not able to play," Colman asked, "or she's not allowed to play?"

"We don't want her to play soccer," Eileen said.

"Why don't you want her to play soccer?"

"It's not a suitable sport for girls."

"It's not an American sport," Ugo said.

"It's not?" Colman said. "Did you know that the American team has won the Women's World Cup and the Olympic women's gold medal more than once?"

"I saw a clip from the final match," Eileen said. "A girl took off her shirt and let everyone in the world see her bra."

Colman shook his head in disbelief. "Is that all you remember about their victory?"

"Yeah, that's all I remember. I was so embarrassed."

"Well, you don't have to worry about Marisol taking off her shirt and letting everyone in the world see her bra."

"You mean Meredith," Ugo said.

"If she plays on a soccer team," Gina said, preempting an argument about the name change, "it'll help her make friends."

From the look in her eyes, Eileen seemed receptive to this benefit: if Marisol made friends, then she could meet the parents of those friends.

"Sports are one of the best ways for kids to make friends," Colman said, adding support.

Ugo said nothing. He had never played a sport, but he had made friends with classmates at the Prep who shared his interest in electronics.

Eileen finally said: "Well, I'll ask about the community soccer teams."

It turned out that the league for girls Marisol's age played in the fall, so there was time for her to try out for a team. When she made the team, Ugo said that every girl who tried out made the team, and when she started in the first match, he said that after they saw her play they would replace her, and when she scored a goal, he said it was a fluke.

On some principle that Gina never understood, he didn't go to another match, and Eileen was left with the task of driving Marisol to matches, along with the other soccer moms. Gina and Colman went to every match, and they found Eileen on the sideline with the mothers of other players, sitting in chairs that could be folded up like umbrellas. Gina and Colman brought chairs that her father had bought years ago for the patio behind the house on Palmer Road. They had woven plastic strips, which had been replaced at least twice, and aluminum frames, which were no longer shiny. Gina could tell that Eileen was embarrassed by those chairs, and for the next match she provided two acceptable chairs for them.

Eileen was in her element among the other women, and she graciously introduced them to Gina and Colman as if they were guests at a party she was having. While Gina and Colman didn't take their eyes off the play, Eileen chatted continuously with the women, who checked the field now and then to see how their children were doing.

Colman hadn't played soccer as a kid because it didn't exist in the neighborhood of the Bronx where he grew up, but he had gotten to know soccer after he went to South America, where it was the most important sport. He had learned to play it, strictly for fun, while he was in Chile serving in the Peace Corps. And for years he had coached a boys' soccer team that played during the summer in Yonkers. So whenever he commented that Marisol had made a good play, he had credibility.

One time after a match in which she had scored three goals, the coach stopped Eileen at her car and said: "Your kid is a natural, so I hope she keeps playing."

In the next to last match of the season a girl from the other team tripped Marisol as she was breaking into the clear, and

Marisol landed hard on the turf, injuring her arm—in fact, later they learned that it was broken. The referee gave the other girl a red card and awarded Marisol a penalty shot, which she made easily, winning the match. But afterward she found the girl who had tripped her and punched her in the face, giving her a bloody nose. It was out of play, so it didn't draw a penalty, but Eileen was humiliated by her daughter's display of such lowlife behavior, which must have been observed by at least some of the women she sat with, so she decided that Marisol wasn't going to play soccer anymore. She informed Gina and Colman of this decision while they were at the table having dinner and Marisol was in the basement watching television.

"You're not going to let her play soccer anymore?" Colman said as if he couldn't believe what he had just heard. "Can you explain why?"

"I don't want my daughter punching other girls in the face."

"Well, I agree that she shouldn't have punched that girl, but I can understand why she did it. The girl kept committing fouls against her."

"I only saw that one time when the girl tripped her."

"The girl pushed her, and held her, and interfered with her every time she had the ball."

"If she did, then why didn't the referee call a penalty sooner?"

"He didn't want to," Colman said. "But he had to on that last foul. It was so obvious."

"Why didn't he want to call a penalty sooner?" Ugo asked.

"He didn't want to offend the spectators."

"What do you mean?"

"I mean Marisol was by far the best player on the field, and the parents of all those white girls didn't like it."

"Are you implying that people in Sudbury are prejudiced?" Eileen said as if the idea was absolutely preposterous.

"I'm not implying it. I'm saying it."

"Well, you don't know this community. You don't live here."

"I think you're prejudiced against the other girl," Ugo said. "I think you imagined the fouls she committed against Meredith."

"I didn't imagine them. I saw them. And you weren't there, so you're not in a position to make a judgment."

"Well, if that girl did interfere with her," Eileen said, "she must have had a reason."

"She did have a reason," Colman said. "She was envious."

"Why would she have been envious?"

"Because Marisol was a much better player."

Ugo was about to insist that the girl's name was Meredith when Gina gave him an evil eye, and he stopped with his mouth ajar.

Ignoring the sibling conflict, Colman turned to Eileen and said: "I think you should let her keep playing soccer. It brings out the best in her."

"I don't agree," Eileen said, shaking her head. "I think it brings out the worst in her."

"You've made that judgment based on one incident."

"It's more than one incident. I don't like the way she behaves when she plays soccer."

"What exactly don't you like?"

"I don't like her being so physical."

"You want her to lie around all day watching television?"

"At least she doesn't get into trouble when she's watching television."

"She didn't get into trouble playing soccer until today."

"Since it happened once, it can happen again."

So Marisol stopped playing soccer, and there was nothing Gina or Colman could do about it. When she visited them Colman could no longer get her to go out to the backyard and play soccer with him because there was no point now. Of course there hadn't been a point before she started playing on a team, but now that she had known the euphoria of competition there was no going back to kicking a ball around for the fun of it.

Two years after resorting to adoption, Eileen announced that she was pregnant. This time she hadn't announced in advance that she and Ugo were trying to have a baby, and she hadn't said anything about being helped by a fertility clinic, which occurred to Gina and Leonora when Eileen delivered twin girls.

Gina offered to go and help her with the babies, but Eileen had her mother to help her, and she told Gina that what would help most was to have Meredith spend more weekends with her and Colman. So the girl came to stay with them more often.

That year for the first time Eileen sent Christmas cards with a family picture, showing the two white babies. The picture didn't include Marisol.

When she returned from brunch with her sister Gina called Vicki at the store to get the name and email address of the guy who managed technology for their company. While looking for this information, Vicki asked if they had found her goddaughter, and Gina replied that the police were still looking for her. After ending the call she went to her computer and sent an email to Eileen with the information she had gotten from Vicki.

That evening, as they were packing for their trip the next day to San Pedro Sula, the doorbell rang. They stopped what they were doing and went downstairs to answer the door, with Colman in the lead and Gina following.

It was Ron and Emilio, as they should have guessed, but from her feeling of disappointment Gina realized that she had hoped it was an angel bringing good news.

"We won't stay long," Ron said apologetically. "We know you have to leave very early tomorrow morning. But we have some information for you."

"Come into the kitchen," Gina said.

The police officers followed her into the kitchen, where they took their usual places at the table. They had become like members of the family, and as Colman had pointed out, they were acting beyond the call of duty. No crime had been committed. Marisol as an adult could go wherever she wanted to, and she didn't fit neatly into any legal definition of a missing person, unless it was as a vulnerable adult.

"Our geek got a signal from her computer," Ron said. "It came today from San Pedro Sula."

"She must have sent a message," Emilio said.

"Can you track the message?" Colman asked them.

"We're trying to," Ron said. "But it's complicated. In fact, I don't understand how it's done."

"Our guess is, she was contacting the guy who lured her there," Emilio said.

"He didn't meet her at the airport?" Gina asked.

"We don't know if he did," Ron said. "If he did, then she was contacting someone else."

"It wasn't us," Colman said. "We've been checking our email regularly."

"I talked again today with the detective there," Emilio said. "He's trying to pick up her trail from the airport."

"Did he confirm that she arrived there?"

"Yeah. He checked with immigration. She entered the country yesterday at one twenty-eight in the afternoon."

"They're evidently good at tracking people who enter the country," Ron said.

Emilio took out a folded paper, saying: "This is the contact information for the detective. He'll expect to hear from you tomorrow afternoon."

"Thanks," Colman said, taking the paper.

"We'll stay in touch with you by cell phone," Ron said. "Be sure to take your chargers."

"Will our phones work there?" Gina asked.

"Oh, yeah. They'll work," Emilio said. "But you'll get hit with roaming charges."

"I don't care about roaming charges," Colman said.

"You need to get some sleep," Ron said, rising purposefully from the table. "Your flight leaves at eight, and you have to be there two hours early."

"All because of eighteen *pendejos*," Emilio said.

"I believe there were nineteen of them."

"Eighteen, nineteen. Think of all the time wasted by millions of people every day because of those nineteen *pendejos*."

"Think of all the jobs they created."

"So they belong with those fat cats who claim they shouldn't pay taxes because of all the jobs they create?"

113

"They belong in the same circle of hell. Now, let's go. These people need to get some sleep."

As she followed the police and her husband to the front door, Gina felt that the techie nerds who had led her goddaughter into the temptations of the virtual world belonged in the same circle of hell with the terrorists and the fat cats.

EIGHT

THEY PACKED BEFORE going to bed that night, and with the help of an alarm clock they got up at four thirty the next morning. The car arrived precisely at five fifteen to take them to the airport. The car service was a local business, the owner of which had come to Colman years ago for advice on structuring his company and still consulted him whenever he had a legal issue. The car was a Crown Victoria, which most of the livery services used, and the driver was a young Latino who attended St. Catherine College, where he was majoring in finance. Colman had taught business law as an adjunct professor at St. Catherine, and he passed the time to the airport talking with the driver about the college's finance program and the professors who taught in it.

Gina hadn't been at the airport since their trip to Punta Cana during the spring break, but from what she could see, they hadn't advanced much in the construction project at the terminal, and they hadn't done anything to make it easier to drop off passengers. Though it was six in the morning, there was a long line of people waiting to check in, and there was an even longer line for security. Following Colman, she took off her shoes and put them into the plastic tray along with her pocketbook, pushed the tray forward, and then entered the station where she was subjected to a body scan. As she raised her arms, she wondered what she looked like to the security person who was examining her for possible terrorist intentions.

Retrieving her shoes and pocketbook from the other side, she saw that they had detected something on Colman, which turned out to be the wooden cross that hung from a lanyard around his neck, inside his shirt. The only metal was the ring that attached the cross to the lanyard, but that had been enough to trigger an alarm.

115

When they were finally cleared they had more than an hour to kill before their flight, so they went to one of the restaurants and had breakfast. Their flight was on time, and it boarded only a few minutes after Colman paid the check at the restaurant.

Their seats were in economy, in the twenty-first row. There was room above for their carry-on luggage, which Colman tucked into the compartment leaving a place for the luggage of a third person. As she settled into the middle seat, with Colman at the window, Gina happily recalled the flight to Punta Cana on which Marisol had sat in the middle, between them. Since the flight didn't have access to the internet, the girl couldn't escape into her computer, and she was available to talk with them.

Gina held Colman's hand from the time the plane began its sprint down the runway to the time it was safely aloft, and then she leaned her head back and closed her eyes.

Shortly after celebrating her ninth birthday Marisol came for a weekend with a plastic pill dispenser. It had seven boxes with lids on them inscribed with the first letters of the days of the week. And when Gina opened the lid of the box for Saturday she saw four different pills.

"What are these pills for?" she asked Marisol.

With a shrug of indifference the girl said: "I don't know. My doctor prescribed them."

"What doctor?" Eileen hadn't mentioned any doctor.

"The doctor I see about my problems."

"What problems?"

"Ask my mother. She thinks I have problems."

"What about you? Do you think you have problems?"

With another shrug the girl said: "I guess I do or my mother wouldn't have sent me to this doctor."

Seething with anger, Gina called Eileen, who as usual didn't answer her phone. She left a message, and while she waited for Eileen to call back, her anger intensified. If the pills had been antibiotics, she would have understood, though she still would have faulted Eileen for not telling her about them. But obviously the girl was seeing a psychiatrist, and if Eileen had told her about it, she would have understood, though she wouldn't have agreed that the girl needed a psychiatrist. A therapist maybe, but not a psychiatrist. She had heard from Leonora's daughter Darcy about how parents were pressured by schools to put their children on behavior-modifying drugs so that they would be easier to manage. This was almost the only thing that Darcy didn't like about being a teacher—the pressure from the school to put children on drugs. So maybe Ugo and Eileen had been pressured by the school in Connecticut to put Marisol on drugs.

When Eileen finally called back, Gina got right to the point, saying: "I see that Marisol is taking pills. What are they for?"

"They're for her problems."

"What problems?"

"For one thing, she has an anger management problem."

"She does? I never saw any evidence of that."

"You only see her when she visits you," Eileen said, "and then she's on her best behavior. You don't see her every day."

"So what evidence have you seen?"

"I haven't seen any myself, but I get reports about her conduct at school."

"You mean from the principal?"

"Yes, and from the school psychologist. I hear from him almost every week. She's always getting into fights."

"With boys or with girls?"

"Always with boys."

"Does she start those fights?"

"That's not the point. She has to learn to manage her anger."

"And a drug will help her learn to manage her anger?"

"A drug will make it easier for her to control her anger."

"And that will help her learn to manage it?"

"We're doing what the doctor recommended."

"I assume this doctor is a psychiatrist."

"Of course he is," Eileen said. "If he wasn't a psychiatrist, he couldn't prescribe medications."

"How did you find him?"

"The school psychologist referred us to him."

"How long has Marisol been seeing him?"

Eileen paused. "About a month."

"That doesn't sound long enough to make a diagnosis."

"Well, he has her whole file from the school psychologist, so he knows her history."

"Does he know her history before she was adopted?"

"There's no way he could possibly know that," Eileen said in his defense. "Even *we* don't know her history before she was adopted. But he knows her recent history."

"So based on her recent history at the school he prescribed a drug to help her learn to manage her anger. What are the other three pills for?"

"One of them is to help her concentrate."

Gina had heard about this drug from Darcy, who said that half of the kids at her school were on it. "Is it Ritalin?"

"It's like Ritalin, but it's something else."

"So this doctor diagnosed Marisol with ADHD?"

"Yes. And he said the drug would help her."

"What are the other two pills for?"

"You don't need to know."

"I do need to know. I'm her godmother."

"That doesn't give you a right to know everything about her."

Seeing that for now she wasn't going to learn anything more about the pills, Gina returned to the subject of the girl's behavior. "Does she get into fights with *your* kids?"

"No. But she does other things."

"What kind of things?"

"She talks disrespectfully to us, and she disobeys us. She's an unruly child."

"So the purpose of these drugs is to pacify her and make her easier to manage?"

"No. That's not the purpose," Eileen said indignantly. "The purpose is to help her."

"Do you think the drugs are helping her?"

"I think they are. She hasn't gotten into a fight since she started taking them, and the school psychologist says her behavior has improved a lot."

"Well, I hope you checked the side effects of these drugs. I heard they can be harmful."

"What do you mean?"

"I mean they can impede normal development of the brain." She was repeating what she had heard from Darcy, who had checked the side effects of all the drugs they gave children to make them easier to manage.

"The doctor assured us that these drugs would have no harmful side effects."

"I'm sure he did. He probably gets kickbacks from the drug companies for prescribing them."

"He wouldn't take kickbacks. He's a reputable doctor."

"That doesn't mean he cares about children."

"I have to go," Eileen said, abruptly ending the conversation. In the background there was a sound of children fighting.

Gina, who was in the kitchen, resisted the urge to throw the pill dispenser into the garbage, having read that with some of these drugs there were harmful effects if you suddenly stopped taking them. Instead, she decided to have a talk with Marisol while they were making dinner together. She planned to make cheese ravioli, and as soon as she had calmed down from her conversation with Eileen she went upstairs to get Marisol.

She found the girl lying on her bed with her computer, staring at its screen.

"What are you doing?" she asked, advancing toward the bed.

"I'm watching an old movie."

"How is it?"

"Boring."

"Then why don't you come down to the kitchen and help me make the ravioli."

The girl sighed as if she didn't have the energy to do anything but lie on the bed in a stupor. "Oh, I don't feel like it."

"Come on," Gina urged her gently. "It's your favorite dish. And it's always better when you help me make it."

The girl typed a command on the keyboard and closed her computer. When she got up she left it on the bed, still turned on.

"Please put your computer on the table," Gina told her. "It's hot, and it might start a fire if you leave it on the bed."

"It's not hot enough to start a fire."

"Do what I ask you, please."

The girl picked up her computer and set it on the table next to the bed.

As they left the room Gina wondered if Marisol had behaved differently in that situation as a result of taking one of those pills. Did she argue less than she had before? And if she had, would that have been desirable? Gina understood that having Marisol for a two-day visit wasn't the same as having to deal with her every day, but she still believed that if she had been in Eileen's position she would never have put the girl on drugs to make her easier to manage.

Back in the kitchen, she asked Marisol to get the ingredients they would need—flour from the cupboard and eggs as well as cheese from the refrigerator—while she got out the rolling pin, a mixing bowl, and the hand-crank ravioli maker.

Marisol, who had been listless, was invigorated by the task of mixing the flour with the eggs and rolling out the dough on the counter.

Watching her, Gina asked: "How's school?"

"It's all right," the girl mumbled.

"Your mother told me you've been getting into fights at school."

The girl kept rolling out the dough as if she hadn't heard this statement.

"Is it true? Have you been getting into fights?"

"Yeah, sometimes. But they deserve it."

"Who deserves it?"

"The boys at school."

"What do they deserve?"

"A punch in the mouth."

"Do they say things that hurt you?"

"Yeah. They call me names."

"What kind of names?"

The girl stopped rolling and rested the pin on the flattened dough. "They call me all kinds of names, but the one that hurts the most is 'greasy spic.' "

"I understand," Gina told her. "In the neighborhood where I grew up there were kids who called me a 'guinea' because I was Italian."

"Did it hurt you?"

"Yeah. It made me feel I didn't belong in the neighborhood."

"That's how I feel when they call me a 'spic,' " Marisol said, looking up from the counter as if she was amazed that someone else could feel what she felt.

"Those boys who call you that name deserve to be punched in the mouth. But even though they deserve it," Gina quickly added, "you shouldn't retaliate against them."

"I know," the girl said. "And I know what Jesus told us to do. I even tried it. Once when a boy called me that name, I turned and walked away. But he kept calling me a 'spic,' shouting louder and louder until everyone could hear him."

"Where did this happen?"

"On the playground."

"And the teacher didn't stop him?"

"There wasn't a teacher. There was only the woman who works in the office of the school psychologist, and she doesn't care what happens on the playground."

"Tell me about the school psychologist. What's he like?"

"I don't know. He thinks he understands me, but he really doesn't. And he only pretends to listen when I tell him how I feel."

"What do you tell him?"

"I tell him they never should have taken me away from my mother."

"But they didn't take you away from your mother. She died in a car accident."

"That's what they told me. And most of the time I believe it, but at times I don't—especially when the boys call me a 'spic.' "

"I understand. They make you wish you were back in your home country."

"Yeah. They make me feel I don't belong here."

"Well, as far as I know," Gina said after a silence, "your mother did die in a car accident. So they didn't take you away from her. They took you away from the orphanage where you were living at the time."

"And they gave me a home. I know the story." The girl lifted the dough and fed it into the machine. As she turned the crank she asked: "Did you ever punch a boy in the mouth?"

"No. I felt like doing it, but something always stopped me."

"What stopped you?"

"Knowing it would hurt my hand."

Marisol laughed as if she had expected a different answer. She rarely laughed, and it was good to hear her laugh. But after dinner, while the three of them were playing a card game, Gina couldn't help thinking about what Marisol had told the school psychologist. Of course it was something he didn't want to hear. In his position he didn't want trouble, and he was willing to use drugs if they stopped kids from causing it.

When she told Colman about the drugs he was absolutely livid. It took a lot to make him angry, but hearing about injustices suffered by people who had no power, especially children, always made him angry. Though it was late at night, he called Eileen and demanded to know the names of all the pills that Marisol was taking, and when Eileen refused to tell him, he threatened to report her to social services. Of course it was an empty threat because he didn't believe that a state government bureaucracy would interfere with the right of parents to put their children on medications that were legally prescribed by doctors. But the next morning he started doing research on cases involving the medication of children in the hope of finding a precedent that he could use to make Eileen give him the names of the drugs.

They thought of asking Marisol to get this information from the pill bottles. But they realized that she probably didn't have access to the bottles because they should have been kept out of reach of children. And anyway they had qualms about using the child for this purpose.

They did get from Marisol the name of the psychiatrist who was treating her, and Colman checked him on the internet, hoping to find things about him that they could use to convince Eileen to let the girl see another doctor for a second opinion. The comments from patients weren't all positive, and there had been one lawsuit for malpractice, which was settled out of court, but there wasn't enough to make a strong case because in Colman's experience you could find such things about almost any doctor.

Gina still felt it was worth trying to persuade Eileen to let Marisol see another doctor for a second opinion, so she called Eileen and made her own case, which she based on the possible side effects of the drugs. Eileen, who didn't seem closed to the idea of getting a second opinion, said she would discuss the matter with Ugo and get back to her. The next evening Eileen called back and said that Ugo was adamantly opposed to the idea. When Gina asked what his reasons were for taking this position, Eileen said that Ugo didn't have to justify it: he was the father.

After more than a week of research Colman found a case that might have been applicable. It involved a man who took legal action against his sister for putting her twelve-year-old daughter on weight-loss pills that had possible negative side effects. The plaintiff's goal was to gain custody of the child, but when he won, the mother appealed, and the case dragged on for years. By the time it went to trial again the girl had lost weight by eating less and by exercising more, so there was no cause for taking her away from her mother.

The lesson learned from this case was that they shouldn't try to help Marisol by taking legal action against her parents because it could do more harm than good. Instead, they talked with a therapist, a neighbor of Leonora, in the hope of learning more about the kind of problems that Marisol had been diagnosed with.

They met informally one evening at Leonora's house, where the therapist, whose name was Susan, began the conversation by stating that too many kids were being put on drugs. She said that all parties were to blame: parents who lacked the patience to deal with kids that didn't meet their expectations, teachers who wanted kids that were easier to manage, psychiatrists who were all too ready to prescribe drugs, and pharmaceutical companies that pushed the drugs.

"So who cares about the children?" Gina asked.

"There are parents and teachers who care about the children."

"What about psychiatrists and pharmaceutical companies?"

"There are good psychiatrists," Susan said, "but too many of them have sold out to Big Pharma, which makes it worth their while to prescribe drugs—and also funds research to show that the drugs are effective."

"We don't have authority over this kid," Colman said, "so we can't even find out what drugs they put her on."

"We know one of them," Gina said. "They put her on a drug like Ritalin."

Susan frowned. "Too many kids are on those drugs, and not just the kids whose doctors prescribe them. Kids who have a supply of those drugs sell them to other kids, who want to enhance their performance on tests."

"Really? Are they like the drugs that athletes take to enhance their performance?"

"They're different, but they serve the same purpose."

"Do they have serious side effects?"

"Some kids have allergic reactions to them. How long has she been on the drug?"

"For about a month."

"Then she's probably not allergic to it. But they also cause stomach pain, nausea, vomiting, and loss of appetite."

Gina reflected. "She hasn't complained about stomach pain or nausea, but she does seem to have lost her appetite."

"Does she have vision problems or dizziness?"

"Not that we know of."

"What about sweating or skin rash?"

"She sweats a lot. Her body runs at a high temperature."

"Does she have sleep problems?"

"I think she does. She stays up late on her computer."

Susan nodded as if she had heard this observation many times. "Has she lost any weight?"

"I don't think so."

"It's probably too soon for that effect. But you should watch for these effects."

"And what if we notice them?" Colman asked.

"You can tell the parents. Maybe they'll listen to you."

"Maybe they will, but so far they haven't."

Susan paused to think about the situation. "You said she's taking four different pills. Do you know what the others are for?"

"We know that one is for anger management," Gina said.

"There are no specific drugs for anger management, but her psychiatrist could have put her on an antidepressant. There are a lot of antidepressants, and they all have possible side effects. They're also addictive, so you can't just stop taking them."

"Do you have any idea what the other two drugs could be?" Colman asked.

"They could be anything. When patients have a problem for which there's no specific drug, the doctors often try a drug that was developed for another purpose. And if that drug doesn't work, they try another."

"You mean they use trial and error?"

"It's a valid scientific method."

"Maybe it's valid for experiments on rats," Gina said, "but not on children."

"I'm with you there," Susan said. "Too many people don't realize that being a parent or a teacher takes patience. They want instant results, which they think they can get by using drugs. And drugs can do irreparable harm."

"That's all the more reason," Colman said, "why we should get a second opinion. But we have no legal right to intervene."

"I can understand your frustration," Susan said.

"Do you have any advice for us?" Gina asked.

"My only advice is to keep trying to convince the parents to get a second opinion. They just might find a psychiatrist who cares about children. And keep loving Marisol. Be patient with her, be kind to her."

Their plane landed on time in Miami, and then they had to wait almost two hours for their connecting flight to San Pedro Sula. They killed time walking around the airport and sharing a Cuban sandwich at a restaurant and reading the *Miami Herald* in the waiting area. A story about how a Miami jury found a man guilty of sex trafficking roused the fear that had tormented Gina since the evening Marisol had gone missing.

It took about two and a half hours to fly from Miami to San Pedro, and it took about an hour and a half to get off the plane, retrieve their luggage, find a taxi, and go to their hotel, which was located near the city center, one block south of Boulevard Morazán. Their room was on the third floor, and it had a connection to the internet.

The first thing Colman did after unpacking was to email Ron and let him know they had arrived—and to ask him if there was any news. Within fifteen minutes Ron responded thanking him for his message and saying there was no news.

Then he called the police officer whom Emilio had talked with. His name was José Peralta, and he was an inspector. It took him more than two hours to return the call, and while they waited to hear from him they used Gina's phone to call the orphanage and arrange a meeting that evening with Sister Eugenia.

After some discussion Peralta agreed to meet with them at four thirty. They took a taxi to the address he gave them, and they were stopped at the entrance to the building, where a guard examined their passports and scanned their faces to make sure they were who they claimed to be and then finally let them go in.

A young woman in uniform led them to an office, where they found Peralta, a lean man with a face that looked as if it was carved out of tropical hardwood, talking energetically on the phone. Without missing a beat in his rapid-fire conversation he motioned for them to sit down in the two folding chairs in front of his desk. Despite his heavy barrage of words he seemed to be fighting a losing battle with the person he was arguing with.

"*Qué cabrón,*" he said, ending the call. "*No sabe lo que mierda que está haciendo.*"

Colman said nothing, but he nodded sympathetically.

"You understand Spanish?"

"Yes, we do."

"I'm sorry. You'll have to excuse my ill-mannered language," Peralta said to Gina.

"*No hay problema,*" Gina said. "I've heard a lot worse."

Peralta looked at her and then at Colman as if he was coming out of a daze. "You came here to find your daughter, right?"

"Our goddaughter," Colman said.

"A Dominican police officer in your country asked me to verify that she entered our country. I did that for him, but I don't know what else you expect me to do."

"We expect you to help us find her."

Peralta leaned forward combatively. "Do you know what's happening in our country?"

"I have an idea," Colman said.

"We've been taken over by drug lords. They're using our country to ship about eighty percent of the cocaine that goes to your country. They're killing people every day. In fact, in this city more than three people on average are killed every day. And you expect me to take the time to look for a missing teenage girl?"

"If you find her, you could prevent a murder."

"Yeah, if I find her alive." Peralta leaned back and folded his arms. "From what I remember of my conversation with that Dominican, your goddaughter is of legal age and she came to our country voluntarily."

"That's right," Colman said.

"Then why do your police take the time to look for her? No crime has been committed, and they must have other things to do."

"They have a lot of other things to do. But I've helped them in the past, and now they're helping me."

"What's your profession?"

"I'm a lawyer. I work for our community, and I help kids who get into trouble."

"Kids who join gangs?"

"Oh, yeah. We have gangs in our city."

"But you don't have a murder rate as high as ours."

"It's not as high as yours, but it's unacceptable."

Peralta reflected. "If I help you, will you return the favor?"

"It depends on what you want in return."

"I don't want money, if that's what you're thinking."

"It's not what I'm thinking. Tell me what you have in mind."

"I have a daughter. She's fifteen. And I want her to live in a better place."

"I work with immigrants," Colman said. "I know the process, and I have to tell you upfront that I couldn't guarantee that your daughter would be able to enter our country. But I could represent your daughter pro bono."

"What do you think her chances would be?"

"It's hard to say. If we could make a case that her life's in danger because her father's a police inspector, then her chances might not be so bad. But the situation has been disrupted by a surge in children fleeing from the violence of this region and appearing at our border and hoping to find refuge in our country."

"What will your country do with those children?"

"We'll turn them away," Colman said. "Our politicians don't care about children."

"Ours don't either," Peralta said. He was silent for a while, and then he said: "Well, my daughter's life *is* in danger. Those animals not only kill police, they kill families. And they target police who are trying to do a good job."

"I assume you're trying to do a good job."

"I am, and I'm not the only one. I know we have corrupt police, but most of us are honest. Most of us want to rid our country of those animals and live in peace. So unless I stop trying to do a good job, they're eventually going to target me."

"Then I'll do my best to get your daughter to a safe place."

Peralta drew his hands down over his face as if he was cleaning the slate of his mind, and then with a notepad in front of him, he asked a methodical series of questions. When they got to the part of how Marisol had presented herself on the internet he slowed down and asked: "You say she was pretending to be a boy?"

"Yeah. We don't understand why, but she does have gender identity issues."

"Did she post any photos of herself online?"

"The police didn't find any."

"So whoever lured her doesn't know what she looks like." Peralta paused, considering this fact. "The question is, what does this person want from her?"

"He could want to use her for commercial sex," Colman said.

"But he doesn't know what she looks like," Peralta said. "She could be fat and ugly. And he thinks she's a boy."

"He could want money from her."

Peralta shook his head. "He would have to set up a way to collect a ransom from you, and that would expose him to the risk of being caught."

"What other use could he have for an eighteen-year-old girl?" Gina asked.

"You mean an eighteen-year-old boy," Colman said.

"Most of the crime in our country," Peralta said, "is related to drugs, so he could have a use for her in that industry."

"Doing what?" Colman asked.

"Working in the channels of distribution into and out of the country. They use kids in that activity because they're expendable."

"But how would he make her do that kind of work?" Gina asked, though she could guess.

"The same way he would make her sell her body—he would threaten to kill her if she didn't do it, and he would beat her up to reinforce the point."

"What you're saying," Colman said, "is that he would make a slave of her."

"Their whole operation is based on slavery," Peralta said. "Cocaine is produced, distributed, and consumed by slaves."

After an uncomfortable silence Colman said: "If you're right about how he wants to use her, then won't he be disappointed to learn that she's a girl?"

"No, they have girls working for them. Girls are especially useful as mules."

Gina understood, and it made her feel sick.

Peralta tapped his pen on the notepad. "Now, let's get back to the fact that the person who lured her doesn't know what she looks like. He had to arrange to meet her somewhere. And he would want to meet her as soon as she entered the country."

"You mean to give her as little time as possible to have second thoughts," Colman said.

"Exactly. So we'll ask the drivers who go regularly to the airport to meet people if they saw your goddaughter being met by someone on—what flight was it?"

Gina gave him the airline, the flight number, and the time of arrival.

"And of course I need a photo of her."

"Didn't Emilio send you a photo?"

"He probably did, but it's buried in my email. It'll save time if you give it to me now."

Gina found the photo she had given to the police in Yonkers and after getting Peralta's phone number she sent it to him.

"She's a beautiful girl," Peralta said, looking at the screen of his phone.

"She is when she smiles," Gina said.

After doing something on his phone, Peralta handed it to Gina, saying: "This is my daughter."

She looked at the photo, touched by the sweetness and innocence of the child. "She looks like an angel. What's her name?"

"María Mercedes. *Es mi tesoro.*"

NINE

AN HOUR LATER they met with Sister Eugenia at the orphanage, an ancient building not far from the city center. They met in an office where the only pieces of equipment were a typewriter and a telephone. They sat in chairs that must have been donated long ago by an estate. The lighting was dim.

Sister Eugenia was a wiry woman with functionally trimmed gray hair. Despite what she must have seen in her ministry, she had a cheerful demeanor, and she welcomed Gina and Colman with a smile that radiated joy.

"You must be tired from your trip," she told them. "Would you like some coffee?"

"No, thanks," Gina said. "I got a little sleep on the plane."

"I haven't been on a plane since the last time I reported to our motherhouse."

"Where is your motherhouse?"

"In Ohio, south of Akron."

"That's a long trip."

"Yes, it is. I used to go more often, but now it's so hard to travel by plane."

"How long have you been here?" Colman asked.

"Almost fifteen years."

"You must have seen a lot of changes."

"I have," Sister Eugenia said. "Mostly for the worse. There's a lot more violence in this country than there was before."

"We've heard there is," Gina said.

"But I never lose hope. There are still a lot of good people in this country."

"We met one of them—a police detective."

"What's his name?"

"José Peralta."

"I know him well. He's a good man. He understands that the girls on the street are victims, not criminals, and he treats them accordingly."

"He agreed to help us find our goddaughter."

"Marisol," the nun said as if she remembered the girl clearly. "Did you know that the name is a shortened form of María de la Soledad?"

"I didn't know that."

"Literally, *soledad* means solitude, but it also means loneliness and desolation and isolation."

"Then her name really fits her."

"Well, it did then. Marisol was the most withdrawn child we ever had, and we've had a lot of withdrawn children."

"How old was Marisol when she came here?" Colman asked.

"She was three years old. She was found on the street by a man who luckily had no evil intentions. He brought her here, holding her hand."

"Do you have his name on record?"

"No. He wouldn't tell us his name. He evidently wanted to do a good deed anonymously."

"What was her condition?"

"She was hungry. The man said he bought her a *baleada* from a street vendor, but she refused to eat it. Her mother must have taught her not to accept food from strangers."

"Well, at least her mother taught her something."

"I guess she did. And the girl trusted us, which suggested that her mother had taken her to church."

"Or been a beggar in front of a church."

"That's possible. In front of a church she would have seen nuns, and she would have had good experiences with them."

"Did her mother ever come here to see her?" Gina asked.

"She came here once when Marisol was around five. She didn't want to acknowledge to the girl that she was her mother. She only wanted to see her, so I didn't tell Marisol that the woman was her mother."

"What happened?"

"Her mother saw her for about five minutes, and then she left. She was in tears."

"Did Marisol notice the tears?"

"No. Her mother turned away from her before she started crying, and she walked straight out and never came back."

"Did you ever tell Marisol that the woman was her mother?"

Sister Eugenia shook her head. "I thought it would have hurt her unnecessarily, and she'd already been hurt enough."

"You mean by being abandoned."

"Yes. Unless you work with these poor kids, you have no idea how much it hurts them to be abandoned. They never get over it. At best they learn to accept it and live with it, but the pain never goes away."

"It sounds like you know how they feel."

"I know from personal experience. I was abandoned by my mother and raised in an orphanage."

Gina didn't know what to say, other than: "So you're the right person for this ministry."

"Maybe I am, and maybe I'm not. I just try to do my best for these children."

After a pause Colman said: "In our phone conversation you said that Marisol resisted being adopted."

"She did. She might have been waiting for her mother to come and get her. Whatever the reason, she refused to be adopted until your sister came along."

"My sister-in-law," Gina said. "She's married to my brother."

"From what I remember, you don't look like her. Well, anyway, Marisol agreed to be adopted by them. She might have thought it was her last chance to be adopted."

"You said you had doubts about them," Colman said.

"I did. I didn't have a feeling that they might use her for an evil purpose, like the men who used her mother. I just had a feeling that she wasn't what they wanted, and that they were taking her because they thought it was their last chance to adopt a child. You know what I mean?"

Gina nodded but refrained from telling the sister that her feeling about them had been right.

"So why did you let her go with them?" Colman asked.

"I felt she'd have a better chance with them than with a couple here who'd take her as a servant. A lot of people here don't treat their servants very well."

"And they did take her out of this country, which is a very dangerous place."

"Don't tell me. Only a few nights ago two guys with automatic weapons broke in and threatened to kill me if I didn't give them all our money. After taking what little money we had, they debated whether to rape me, but they finally decided not to, I guess because I was too old. That's one advantage of being old," the sister added impassively.

"Speaking of rape," Colman said, "do you think it's possible that Marisol was sexually abused while she was on the street?"

"It's possible, and I realize that at her age she might not have been too young for some of those men, but there was no physical evidence of abuse, so I don't think anything happened to her on the street. And nothing happened to her here."

"You said you saw her mother on the street a few years after Marisol came here, and you took her to a lay worker who helped girls in her situation."

"That's right. I hoped that if she was rehabilitated she'd come back and get her daughter. But the next thing I heard about her she was back on the street."

"Was she on drugs?"

"I don't know, but many of those poor girls are on drugs. Their pimps get them addicted, and then they have to sell themselves to pay for the drugs."

"How do you break that vicious circle?" Gina asked.

"With love," Sister Eugenia said.

After a silence Colman asked: "Have you been able to find the lay worker you took her to?"

"Yes, I have her new location. She's the last person I know who was in touch with Marisol's mother, so she might be able to help you find her."

It wasn't long after Marisol's fourteenth birthday when Eileen called and invited Gina and Colman to a family conference in Sudbury. Eileen didn't tell her the reason for it, and Gina had trepidations about it, imagining various scenarios that ranged from Ugo and Eileen getting a divorce to one of their children having leukemia. For some reason she never imagined what it was about, and when Eileen told her as they were sitting in the formal living room that was only used for guests, she realized that she should have seen it coming.

"We've decided to put Meredith in a foster home," Eileen said with her eyes fixed on the coffee table, which displayed a book about Florence.

"What?" Colman said, shocked.

"We've done our best, but we can't handle her. And she's having a very bad influence on our own children at a critical time in their development."

"If you don't want her," Gina said without hesitation, "we'll take her."

"You don't know what you'd be getting into. You only see her when she visits you, and then she's on her best behavior."

"You've said that before," Colman said, "and it was a crock of shit the first time."

"There's no need to use language like that," Eileen said primly.

"You don't seem to understand. This girl isn't a kitten you adopted from an animal shelter, which you can return if you're not happy with it. She's a human being."

"I know she is, but you have no idea what it's like living with her every day."

"And you have no idea," Gina said, "what it was like living with Ugo when he was her age."

"I was a model child," Ugo said with a smirk.

"You were a spoiled brat. And you know what? When our mother, at her wit's end, took you to a doctor and asked him what she should do with you, he advised her to put you on drugs, which of course as a responsible parent she wouldn't do because she was afraid that they would affect your precious brain."

"That's a good story, but it didn't happen."

"It did happen. If you ask Leonora, she'll confirm it."

"Leonora always takes your side," Ugo said, playing the victim.

"The point is," Gina said, "you're perfectly willing to do things to your child that your parents would never have done to you."

"Technically, she's not our child," Eileen said.

"Legally, she is," Colman said. "You adopted her, so you're legally responsible for her."

"The adoption was done in a banana republic," Ugo said. "It's not valid here."

"You claimed you had legal authority to prevent us from getting a second opinion when you put her on drugs, and now you claim you have no legal responsibility?"

"We're only trying to do what's best for her," Eileen said.

Colman shook his head. "You're trying to do what's best for *you*, not for her, and I don't agree that she should go to a foster home. She should live with us."

"But you have no experience with children."

"You never had them," Ugo said with a scornful look at Gina.

Hurt to the core, she retaliated. "I never had children because I devoted my life to our family. I took care of our father until he died, and I took care of you until you were married, so I never had a chance to go on dates. When I got married I was forty-seven, so how was I supposed to have children?"

"You could have gotten knocked up when you were younger."

"Listen," Colman said menacingly, "if you say one more thing like that, I'm going to tear your fucking head off."

"She's my sister. I can say anything I want to her."

"No, you can't. Not in my presence. You understand?"

Ugo made a face, with his lower lip curled over, but he didn't say a word of protest.

"What's best for the girl," Gina said after a silence, "is to live with us. She knows us, and she's used to us. And we're family."

"All right," Eileen said, "but don't say we didn't warn you."

"Now, when are we going to tell the girl what's happening?" Colman asked.

"The sooner, the better," Ugo muttered.

"I think we should tell her we want her to come and live with us," Gina said, "and you should tell her it's best for her."

"You mean we should talk with her together?" Eileen asked as if she didn't think it was a good idea.

"Of course we should," Colman said. "We want her to get a unified message."

"And the message is," Gina said, "that we all agree that Marisol should live with us."

"You mean Meredith," Ugo said.

"If they're going to take her," Eileen told him, "they can call her anything they want. We're done with her."

Eileen asked her adopted daughter to come upstairs and join them. The girl entered the living room as if she was expecting to be punished for something, and she stood mutely in front of the fireplace while Gina as the head of the family told her they had all agreed that she should live with her godmother and her uncle in Yonkers. Marisol seemed to understand that she didn't have any choice in the matter, and her only comment was: "Okay."

Within an hour they had packed her things and were heading for the Merritt Parkway. With her earbuds in place, the girl tuned out to her world of music.

That night, after Marisol got into bed, Gina gave her a hug and said: "You're here because we want you. We love you, and we'll always love you, no matter what happens."

Marisol only allowed the hug, and she said nothing.

Over the next few days they adjusted to the fact that Marisol was living with them permanently, not just visiting, and they had to deal with behaviors that they allowed when she was only there for the weekend, knowing that whatever they did, Marisol would revert to those behaviors as soon as she returned to Sudbury, where she had learned them. One problem was her lack of attention to hygiene. On the weekend visits Gina had made her take a shower before going home, usually by leading her into the bathroom and into the tub. But now they gave her a rule that she had to take a shower at least every other day, which she resisted. They also gave her a rule that she had to change her underwear every day, which she resisted too. It looked like her parents hadn't taught her anything, including where to put her used tampons, which had to be rooted out of the drain when the water backed up in the basement. When that happened, Gina felt like calling Eileen and holding her accountable for not teaching Marisol even the most basic things of daily living, but she realized that it wouldn't serve any purpose other than to give her a chance to vent her frustrations.

Shortly after the girl came to stay with them permanently Gina wrote down the names of the four drugs that Marisol was taking, and one night after the girl had gone to bed she went into her office and spent the next few hours doing research on the drugs.

When she went downstairs she found Colman sitting at his desk, reviewing a file.

He raised his head and he said: "You look like you're on the warpath."

"I *am* on the warpath. I did research on the drugs she's taking."

"Did you find out what they're for?"

"Yeah. One is for ADHD, as we already knew. Another is for depression, as Susan guessed. Another is for bipolar disorder, and the other is for epilepsy."

"Epilepsy? Since when does she have epilepsy?"

"She doesn't, unless it's one of those secrets they've been keeping from us. But I don't think so. When you have epilepsy, you have seizures."

"What do you have when you're bipolar?"

"You have extreme mood swings. It used to be called manic depression."

Colman frowned. "I never noticed any extreme mood swings in Marisol, did you?"

"No. Of course it's possible that the drug prevented her from having extreme mood swings, but I never noticed any before she started taking the drug."

"And I never noticed any seizures."

"So it looks like the doctor was trying these drugs on Marisol to see if they would work for other purposes, as Susan said they do with patients."

Colman nodded. "The other purposes were to pacify her and make her easier to manage."

"It looks that way. Instead of dealing with her, they put her on drugs, and they didn't care about the side effects."

"What are the side effects?"

"It's a long list, and some of them explain Marisol's behavior—like not having any energy, and not having an appetite, and not being able to sleep. Those are the effects they know about, but they don't know about the long-term effects."

"They don't get funding from the drug companies for research on those effects."

"Well, we can reach our own conclusions based on what I've learned, but we need to get a professional opinion. And we also need to keep in mind that three of the drugs are very addictive, so she can't just stop taking them."

"Should we start with Susan?"

"I think we should," Gina said. "I trust Susan, and she already knows the background."

"Then let's make an appointment," Colman said. "I can move anything on my schedule except court appearances."

Two days later they met with Susan at her office in Hastings, which was reputed to have the highest concentration of therapists of any square mile in the county. The office was in a brick building on Broadway, which had its own parking area.

They knew from Marisol that from time to time she had met with therapists recommended by her psychiatrist, but Eileen had said they hadn't been helpful. Marisol put up no resistance to meeting with yet another therapist, though her body language suggested a person in custody as she entered the office building and climbed the stairs to the second floor.

The outer door of Susan's office wasn't locked, so they walked into a reception area and after standing around for a while sat down on a sofa with Marisol in the middle. There was no receptionist, so Gina wondered how Susan would know they were there, but she waited trusting that Susan was in her office, behind the closed door. And finally the door opened and Susan came out to welcome them.

"I'm Susan," she told Marisol. "I'm glad you're here."

Marisol was reserved as she always was with strangers, but she didn't back away. She seemed willing to give this therapist the benefit of a doubt.

They followed Susan into her office, and they sat down on another sofa, again with Marisol in the middle. Susan sat in a casual chair, not directly in front of them but in a corner, at a distance, as if she wanted to give them space.

Addressing the girl, Susan explained: "I'm a neighbor of your godmother's sister, your Aunt Leonora. I'm a therapist, and I work mainly with teenage girls. Your godmother and your uncle have given me some background on you, but I want you to tell me about yourself—without their being present, so you can feel free to tell me anything. Okay?"

"Okay," the girl said in a subdued voice.

"Can I ask them to leave?"

"Yeah, you can."

Responding to a signal from Susan's eyes, Gina and Colman got up, but before leaving she gently laid her hand on Marisol's shoulder and said: "We'll be in the reception area."

With the door of the office closed behind them, they stood around for a while again before sitting down again on the sofa. Gina leaned against Colman, and he put an arm around her reassuringly.

Forty minutes later, which seemed like hours, the door opened and Susan invited them to come in. Marisol was still sitting in the middle of the sofa, looking unusually peaceful, and they took their places on each side of her.

"I think we had a good talk," Susan said, not to them but to Marisol. "What do you think?"

Marisol nodded definitely.

"Among other things, we talked about the drugs you're taking.

Would you like to tell your godmother and your uncle what you decided?"

"Yeah. I want to see another doctor."

"That's fine," Gina said. "We'll get you another doctor."

"And I don't want to take so many pills."

"Well, let's see what your new doctor says."

"I can recommend a psychiatrist who I think would be perfect for her," Susan said. "She works with teenage girls, and she speaks Spanish."

"Where's she from?" Colman asked.

"She's from Santiago, Chile. She was born and raised there, but she came here to go to medical school, and she stayed here. Her office is in Tarrytown, and she's affiliated with Phelps Memorial Hospital in Sleepy Hollow."

"Would you like to meet with her?" Gina asked Marisol.

"Yeah. I like it that she speaks Spanish."

The lay worker, Celia Jimenez, agreed to meet with them at nine that evening. Her office was outside of the city, and after resting and eating dinner they engaged a taxi in front of their hotel to take them there. On the way they noticed areas that were packed with poor people living in shacks on narrow streets. There were only sporadic lights in these areas, but a beautiful full moon overhead revealed the squalor.

Celia's office was on the main floor of a three-story building. When the door opened, they were greeted by a woman in her mid-thirties with tied-back hair, an open face, and empathetic eyes. She was dressed in loose-fitting jeans and a blue tee shirt that said in white letters: "*Dios te ama.*"

Her office had a work area with a desktop computer and a sitting area with a sofa and four chairs, all of them worn from years of use. Through an open door, Gina detected a living area, so the woman evidently, like Coleman, worked where she lived.

"Thanks for meeting with us," Gina said when they had sat down on the sofa.

"I'd do anything for Sister Eugenia," Celia told them. "She's my role model."

"Did you work with her?"

"I worked with her at the orphanage when I got out of college. I was looking for a mission, and I found it there."

"How did you find it?"

"A family that had adopted a girl from the orphanage reported her as missing when she was thirteen. With the help of the police we found her working on the street as a prostitute. Since her family wouldn't take her back after they learned what she'd been doing, and since she didn't belong in the orphanage at her age, we didn't know what to do with her. So I founded a center to help girls in her situation."

"I imagine it's not easy to help them," Gina said.

"It's not easy," Celia said. "At first they're glad to get away from their pimps, who abuse them, but after a while they miss the life. They especially miss the money they can make from selling their bodies. And they get bored with going to school and learning a trade. So some of them go back to the street, as the mother of your goddaughter did."

"She got bored with going to school?"

"Yes. She didn't have the motivation to stick it out."

"How long was she here?"

"About fifteen months. But we weren't here then, we were at the old address."

"When she left your center," Colman said, "did she tell you where she was going?"

"No. She just left. But I guessed where she'd gone, and I found her there, and I tried to get her to come back for the sake of her daughter."

"You knew she had a daughter?"

"Oh, yes. She often talked about her daughter. She even went to see her once."

"That's what Sister Eugenia told us. How long after she saw her daughter did she leave your center?"

Celia paused to think. "It was about two months later. I noticed that after her visit to the orphanage she worked very hard, and I hoped it had given her motivation. But then she slacked off and finally gave up."

"So you saw her on the street not long after she left your center. Did you see her after that?"

"I did, from time to time. I go into the city every week, and I walk around looking for girls we might help."

"Isn't that dangerous?" Gina asked.

"It's gotten more dangerous. Before, I only had to worry about being attacked by pimps, but now I have to worry about being attacked by gangs, who have more serious weapons than the pimps ever had. But they're not going to scare me off."

"Do you remember," Colman asked, "the last time you saw her on the street?"

Celia paused again to think. "It was about two years ago. I remember because that day I talked a girl into coming with me, and now she's working in a hotel."

"Do you know the name of her pimp?"

"Yes. I know all their names. And you'll have no trouble finding him."

"We won't? Why not?"

"He's in prison for killing one of his girls."

"I assume it wasn't Marisol's mother."

"If it was, I would have told you. But that doesn't mean her mother's alive," Celia added. "Girls on the street don't last long. If their pimps don't kill them, diseases do. A lot of them have HIV or worse."

"There are worse diseases?"

"Yes, there are. But you don't need to know about them. What you need to know is the name of her mother's pimp and his current address."

Celia went over to her desk and got a piece of paper, which she handed to Gina.

"Will our taxi driver know where this is?" she asked.

"You can't see him without the police," Celia said.

"We're working with the police," Colman said.

"Who are you working with?"

"Inspector Peralta."

"He's a good man. He'll help you."

"We think whoever lured our goddaughter here is planning to use her in some way," Gina said. "So how could he use her?"

"He could put her on the street."

"But he would have thought she was a boy."

"That wouldn't make any difference to him. Girls, boys—they have only one use, and that's to be exploited by older people."

"From what I've seen," Coleman said, "I agree. But luckily there are people like you who want to help them."

"I try, but at times I feel like I'm fighting a tidal wave."

"At times I do too, but we have to keep fighting."

In a gesture that she must have learned from watching American sports, Celia offered her palm to them, and they responded one after the other by clapping her palm.

TEN

IT WAS AFTER eleven by the time they returned to their hotel, and exhausted from the trip and the meetings, they crashed into bed. For the first time since Marisol had gone missing, Gina didn't have much trouble falling asleep.

They met with Peralta at nine the next morning, and they reported what they had learned from their conversation with Celia.

"You did well," Peralta said, complimenting them.

"This is the name of the mother's pimp," Colman said, handing a piece of paper to Peralta, "and the name of the prison where he's serving time."

Peralta scanned the paper, frowning. "I remember this guy. He brutally tortured one of his girls, and then he killed her, as a warning for his other girls."

"You mean a warning not to leave him?" Gina asked.

"Yeah, and not to cheat him. The pimps use terror to keep their girls in line. They make slaves of them."

"But according to Celia, some of them go back to their pimps voluntarily."

"I don't think they go back voluntarily, any more than people go back voluntarily to addictive drugs. They get hooked on the life, and it's not easy to break the habit."

"How soon can we talk with this guy?" Colman said, refocusing the conversation.

"In a few hours," Peralta said. "But I don't think you should join me. For one thing, it might inhibit him, and for another thing, you don't need to know what it's like in our prisons."

"That wouldn't bother me. I've been in prison."

"You have?" Peralta looked concerned. "What for?"

"For protesting against Pinochet."

146

"Pinochet? That must have been years ago."

"It was thirty-six years ago."

"How long did they hold you?"

"For eleven weeks."

Peralta exhaled in a long sigh. "What did they do to you?"

"They beat me, they held my head under water, and they put me in a cell that was so small I couldn't stand up in it."

"We don't torture our prisoners now, but we did in the past."

"You mean under your military governments?"

"Yes. It was bad under those governments, but a lot of people think it's worse now. They say at least with the military we had law and order."

"What do you say?"

"I say we need a balance," Peralta said, "between law and order and individual freedom. But now we don't have either. We've been overrun by criminal organizations that defy our laws and subjugate our people."

"Well, at least that pimp was sent to prison."

"He wasn't a member of a big enough gang. If he had been, he never would have gone to prison."

"So let's assume he has some information about Marisol's mother," Colman said after a pause. "What would be his incentive to give it to us?"

"We could offer to make his life in prison a little easier."

"Nothing more?"

"No, nothing more. We're not going to lighten his sentence."

Colman nodded. "That's another reason why we shouldn't join you. I'm an officer of the law, but I'm also the uncle of this girl, so I'd have a conflict between my professional standards and my personal feelings."

"I understand," Peralta said. "And I respect you for saying that. But keep in mind that my personal feelings will be on your side, and I'll do everything within the law to find out whatever that animal knows about the girl's mother."

"That's all we can ask," Gina said.

"Have your learned anything from the drivers at the airport?" Colman asked.

"We only started questioning them after our meeting yesterday, so there hasn't been much time. I got a report this morning, and it had nothing. But I'll get another report at noon, and if it has anything I'll let you know."

They left the police station wondering how to kill the time until they heard from Peralta. They had no more local people to talk with, and they couldn't do anything on their own. They stopped at an outdoor café and ordered espressos, and while they sat there Gina checked for text messages. But there was nothing from Marisol. Colman then called Ron to see if there had been any developments at that end, but there hadn't been any. The locus of the investigation had shifted to San Pedro Sula.

They walked around the city for a while just to get some exercise, and then they returned to their hotel, where they killed time watching the news on television. After one cycle they turned it off, and Gina stretched out on the sofa with her head on Colman's lap.

The psychiatrist, Dr. Rivas, had her office on the second floor of a building on Main Street in Tarrytown, not far from the Music Hall. Like Susan, she had a reception area but there was no one to greet patients, so they sat down in separate chairs and waited until the doctor emerged from her office with a girl who looked like she was in her late teens. They were speaking in Spanish.

After accompanying the girl to the door, Dr. Rivas turned and introduced herself. She was an attractive woman in her mid-forties. She had dark hair that was held back by an aquamarine clamp and dark eyes that were serious but not without an element of humor. She was fashionably dressed, with accessories that included a necklace of aquamarine stones. She invited them to come into her office, where they sat down on a sofa with Marisol in the middle, a pattern that was beginning to seem meaningful.

"Do you all speak Spanish," Dr. Rivas asked.

"They're both fluent in Spanish," Gina said. "I speak an Italian version of it."

"But she's not an Argentine," Colman said in Spanish.

Dr. Rivas cocked her head and said: "You sound like you're from Chile."

"I'm not. I'm from the Bronx. But I lived in Chile for more than three years."

"Really? What were you doing there?"

"I was in the Peace Corps."

"Were you in Santiago?"

"No. I was in Talcahuano and Concepción."

"When were you there?"

"In the mid-1970s."

"That was a bad time," Dr. Rivas said gravely.

"Yeah. It was," Colman said without further comment.

Gina sensed that the doctor would have liked to hear more about Colman's experience in Chile, but they weren't here to talk about Colman.

"Now, we'll talk together for a while," Dr. Rivas said, "and then Marisol and I will talk. Okay?"

"Okay," the three of them said.

"Your therapist, Susan, referred you to me," Dr. Rivas said to Marisol. "How are things going with you and her?"

"They're going okay," Marisol said.

"She told me you don't want to take so many pills. Is that correct?"

Marisol nodded. "I just don't understand why I need them."

"Well, I have your file from the doctor who prescribed them, and I understand why he thought you need them, but I'm going to form my own opinion. That'll take at least a few meetings with you, so don't expect anything to happen overnight."

"How often do you want to meet with her?" Gina asked.

"To get started, twice a week, and then we can meet once a week. Is that okay with you?" Dr. Rivas asked Marisol.

"Yeah, that's okay," Marisol said.

"Then let me establish some basic rules. When all of us talk, everything is out in the open, but when Marisol and I talk, everything is in confidence. Without her permission I can't tell you anything she said to me. *Está claro?*"

"*Sí, está claro*," Colman said.

"As I understand it," Dr. Rivas said to Gina, "you're Marisol's godmother, and her adoptive father is your brother."

"That's right."

"And Marisol came to live with you about a month ago."

"That's right. But she's spent weekends with us since she was adopted."

"How long ago was she adopted?"

"About seven years ago."

"Okay. You must have concerns about her or we wouldn't be here. So could you tell me your concerns?"

Gina hesitated, conscious of the girl's presence.

"When we talk together, everything's out in the open," Dr. Rivas reminded her.

Instead of referring to Marisol in the third person, Gina addressed her directly, saying: "Well, you act like you don't want to do anything, and like you don't want to be with people. You go into your room and close your door and spend hours on your computer."

"Is that a recent development?" Dr. Rivas asked.

"No. It started about five years ago after her parents put her on drugs. Before that she was more engaged."

"You used to play soccer," Colman said.

"I stopped playing soccer before that," Marisol said.

"Were you good at soccer?" Dr. Rivas asked.

Marisol shrugged. "I don't know. I guess I wasn't bad."

"So why did you stop playing soccer?"

"My mother didn't want me to play soccer. She said it brought out the worst in me."

"A girl deliberately tripped her in a soccer match," Colman said. "When she fell, it broke her arm. At the time she didn't know her arm was broken, and she kept playing. But after the match she found the girl and punched her in the face."

"The girl had repeatedly fouled her," Gina said, "and the referee didn't do anything about it until she finally give her a red card for tripping Marisol. So I think Marisol was taking justice into her own hands."

"Is that what you were doing?" Dr. Rivas asked Marisol.

Marisol shrugged again. "I guess I was. The referee should have done something sooner."

Dr. Rivas paused. "Okay. You heard the concerns of your godmother and your uncle. Do you understand their concerns?"

"No, I don't understand why they care if I go into my room and close the door and spend hours on my computer."

"We want you to be with us," Gina said. "Not all the time, but more than you are."

"Do you want to be with them?" Dr. Rivas asked.

"I guess I do. But I don't know why they want to be with me."

"We love you," Gina said. "That's why."

Marisol looked skeptical.

Dr. Rivas gave her a chance to talk, but she clammed up and folded her arms and stared at nothing, rocking back and forth.

"I think this would be a good time for Marisol and me to talk," Dr. Rivas said.

So they left and went to the reception area and sat down.

"What do you think of her?" Colman asked.

"I like her," Gina said.

After four meetings with Marisol the doctor gave them a preliminary opinion without the girl being present. She didn't believe that Marisol had bipolar disorder or epilepsy, but she explained why the previous doctor had diagnosed her with those disorders: he could prescribe drugs for them, and the healthcare plan would pay for them. Professionally, he could justify using those drugs for Marisol's disorder because other doctors were doing the same thing. There were even studies, financed by the drug companies, which showed that those drugs could be effective in treating disorders that they hadn't been designed to treat. But they weren't helping Marisol. They were only suppressing the symptoms of the real problem.

Dr. Rivas believed that the real problem was that as a result of being abandoned by her mother and living in an institution until she was almost seven, Marisol had reactive attachment disorder. The symptoms of this disorder included not establishing healthy attachments with parents or caregivers, not engaging in social interaction, not asking for support or assistance, and not responding to offers of comfort. Children with this disorder avoided physical contact, preferred social isolation, and shunned relationships with virtually everyone.

Since there was no specific drug to treat this disorder, doctors came up with other diagnoses for which they could prescribe drugs, such as anxiety, depression, or hyperactivity. But drugs weren't an effective treatment for this disorder. The only effective treatment was to give Marisol a safe and stable living condition, encourage her to have positive interactions with people, and help her to build a core of self-worth. In other words, there was no quick fix. There was only the long, hard road that parents had traveled from time immemorial.

"You have to remember," Dr. Rivas warned them. "Marisol has no core of self-worth, no memory of being loved and valued. Oh, I'm sure the sisters in the orphanage did their best with her, but no one can undo the damage that was done to her when she was abandoned by her birth mother."

"What about the damage that was done to her when she was abandoned by her adoptive parents?" Gina asked.

"No one can undo that either. It didn't hurt her as much because she wasn't attached to them, but it did make things worse for her. I mean, she's been abandoned twice."

"If no one can undo the damage, then she'll always suffer from this disorder?"

"Unfortunately, yes. There's a void in her that can never be filled completely."

"So what can we do for her?"

"You can help her build a core of self-worth, though it won't be easy because there's nothing to start with."

"Well, how do you help a child build a core of self-worth?" Colman asked.

"How did your mother help you build one?"

"She loved me unconditionally."

Dr. Rivas nodded. "That's the only way. Therapy can help her, but whether or not she builds a core of self-worth will depend a lot on you."

"Do you have any advice for us?" Gina asked.

"Yes. Love is patient, love is kind. Love does not insist on its own way."

Continuing the quotation, Gina said: "Love bears all things, believes all things, hopes all things, endures all things."

"Love never fails," Colman concluded.

"Then you know what it takes," Dr. Rivas told them softly. "God bless you."

Marisol couldn't just suddenly stop taking the drugs that had been administered to her, so Dr. Rivas recommended putting her on a temporary drug that would help her get off the drugs for bipolar disorder and epilepsy. That would take up to three months, and then they could address the drug for depression, which would be the most difficult to get off.

Marisol began a schedule of seeing both her doctor and her therapist once a week. She was still under her mother's healthcare plan, but Dr. Rivas and Susan were out of network, so there was no coverage until the out-of-pocket expenses reached a thousand dollars, and after that there were reimbursements for fifty percent of approved expenses. Gina and Colman together earned less than Ugo, but she knew they would have to absorb the expenses and wait for partial reimbursement after they reached a thousand dollars. It blew a large hole in their budget, but they made the necessary sacrifices.

The process was for Gina to mail checks to Eileen to pay the monthly bills of the doctor and the therapist so that the expenses could be recorded by her healthcare plan. Eileen was supposed to pay the bills within a few days of receiving the money, but two months after they began the process Gina got an email from Dr. Rivas asking if they could at least pay something toward her first bill. Knowing that the two checks for a thousand dollars each that she had sent to Eileen with copies of the doctor's bills had cleared within a few days of their being mailed, Gina emailed Eileen asking if she had paid the bills from Dr. Rivas. An hour later she got a reply saying yes, she had paid the bills, though she didn't say when. It made Gina wonder if Eileen had paid Susan's bills, so she emailed Susan and learned that the therapist hadn't been paid either. It looked like Eileen was delaying payment of these bills and using the money she received for them to pay other expenses. Since the expenses for Marisol wouldn't be recorded by the healthcare plan until Eileen paid these bills, then it would take longer to reach the amount of out-of-pocket expenses above which there would be reimbursements. In fact, they were already well over that amount, so by now there should have been some reimbursements in the pipeline.

A week later she received emails from Dr. Rivas and Susan saying that their bills for the first month of treatment had been paid, and from then on the bills were paid regularly, a month late, but after four months there were still no reimbursements. At that point she called Eileen to find out what was happening.

"It takes them three months to process the payments," Eileen explained.

"It's been four months," Gina said.

"Not since you reached fifteen hundred dollars of expenses."

"I thought the amount was a thousand dollars."

"No, it's fifteen hundred."

After making a quick calculation, Gina said: "At this point our out-of-pocket expenses are six thousand four hundred dollars."

"Then I should get a reimbursement soon."

A few days later Gina received a check in the mail from Eileen, which made her wonder if Eileen had received the money from the insurance company a while ago and was using it to pay other expenses.

From then on she received a check from Eileen every month, but she figured that by delaying payments of the bills for Marisol's treatment and delaying payments for the reimbursements, Eileen was enjoying a float of more than three thousand dollars.

"It's annoying," Colman said after hearing her explain how Eileen was taking advantage of them. "But there's nothing we can do about it. We want Marisol to get the treatment she needs, and we can live with being out of pocket for that amount."

"We're actually out of pocket for that amount plus fifteen hundred dollars," Gina pointed out.

"I know, but the fifteen hundred is a sunk cost."

From the accounting courses that the printing company had paid for, Gina remembered that a sunk cost was a cost that you have already incurred which can no longer be recovered by any means, and that you should not consider sunk costs in making a decision whether to continue investing in a project. That helped her accept the situation, though there was absolutely no question about whether they should continue investing in Marisol.

By then it was September, and they had already paid the tuition for Sacred Heart High School. They had enrolled Marisol there because they believed that she needed the extra attention she would get at a private school. And both of them had gone to private schools, with their parents making sacrifices to give them a Catholic education, so there was no question about whether they should make such an investment in Marisol.

Colman drove her to school in the morning, and from their conversations in the car he reported that she liked Sacred Heart a lot better than the school in Sudbury. She evidently felt more comfortable in a more diverse environment, though she didn't put it that way. She simply said it was better not being the only kid who wasn't white.

At their first meeting with the school counselor they learned that Marisol was doing all right in her courses, and that she was behaving well. The counselor's main concern was that she didn't mix with the other students, and she didn't seem to have made any friends. They talked about possible ways of getting her to interact socially, which they had talked about with Susan. The problem was getting Marisol to do any of those things.

They had thought of having her resume playing soccer, but she hadn't played in more than five years, and they didn't want her to make a bad first impression on the girls who might become her friends. So during the summer Colman had her start working out with the team he coached. They were boys between the ages of twelve and thirteen, so she wasn't much older than they were, and she was about the same size as they were. After a while the boys didn't seem to notice that she was a girl. She still had the talent she was born with, but she was out of practice and out of shape, and she didn't have the edge she had before. It was as if the drugs had blunted her skills.

Colman took the long view that working out with the boys was only a step toward getting her back into shape so that she could join a team on which she belonged, and he was extremely patient with her. Of course she never got to play in a match because the other team would have objected, not only because she was a girl but also because she was older.

By the end of October she was no longer taking the drug that helped her get off the drugs for bipolar disorder and epilepsy, so Dr. Rivas was ready to address the drug she was taking for depression. She planned to reduce the dosage by small increments, month to month, and see how Marisol was responding. If all went well, Marisol would be off the drug by the end of six months. But all did not go well. After two months she began having severe antidepressant withdrawal symptoms, which included headaches, body aches, anxiety, and insomnia. She complained most about the headaches, saying it felt like her brain was being zapped. She had even less energy than usual, and more problems with her schoolwork. And then one night she woke up screaming from a nightmare.

"Tell me about it, honey," Gina said, sitting on edge of the girl's bed and rubbing her back.

"It was horrible," Marisol cried.

"Do you remember anything about it?"

"There was a woman. She could have been my mother. They were torturing her."

"Well, I can understand why that was horrible. But it was a nightmare. It didn't really happen."

"It felt like it was really happening."

"I know. Do you remember anything more?"

"No. And I'm forgetting what I did remember."

"That's a blessing of nightmares. They fade away."

"But what if it comes back?"

"I'll be here with you."

She spent the rest of the night in a chair, next to the bed, ready to comfort Marisol if she had another nightmare.

Dr. Rivas kept Marisol on the same dosage of the drug until her withdrawal symptoms abated, and then she resumed reducing the dosage. It took until spring for her to get completely off the drug, and it took until the beginning of summer for her to stop having withdrawal symptoms.

Colman had experience with kids who had gotten off heroin, and he said that what Marisol went through was as bad as what those kids went through.

Shortly before school started that fall they met with Dr. Rivas to review the process of getting Marisol off the drugs. They talked about how difficult it had been for Marisol, and about the possible long-term effects of being on those drugs for five years.

"For one thing," Dr. Rivas said, "they stunted her growth. I can't prove it, but based on the few studies that have been done, I believe she'll be as much as two inches shorter than she would have been without the drugs."

"Is that a serious problem?" Gina asked.

"No. The serious problem is what those drugs might have done to the development of her brain." Dr. Rivas paused. "As you may or may not know, the part of the brain where we feel fear develops earlier than the part of our brain where we manage fear. The latter part, which is called the prefrontal cortex, may not fully develop until we're in our mid-twenties, or even later in some cases. So teenagers have problems in managing fear, and when they have continuing fear for no apparent reason, we say they have anxiety."

"Does that explain why parents have such problems with teenagers?"

"Yes, it does. So parents need to understand that it's perfectly normal for teenagers to behave in ways that look crazy to adults, and that drugs aren't an effective way of dealing with those behaviors. In fact, there's growing evidence that the drugs that parents use to control the behavior of their teenage children only make things worse. In other words, some of those drugs may actually retard development of the prefrontal cortex, extending the period when children behave like teenagers."

"You think those drugs retarded the development of Marisol's brain?" Colman asked.

"I have no evidence that they did," Dr. Rivas said carefully. "But I would say that at the very least they didn't promote the development of her brain."

"If they did retard its development, can her brain catch up?" Gina asked.

"There's a lot of evidence that our brains can overcome such effects, so let's be hopeful that her brain will catch up. But you should be prepared for a long period of transition between her acting like a teenager and acting like an adult."

"We're not in any hurry," Colman said.

"As long as we understand what's happening, we can deal with it," Gina said.

They jumped when Colman's phone rang. It was Peralta, calling to bring them up to date.

"Can I put you on speaker?" Colman asked with his finger poised over the button. The answer must have been affirmative because Colman turned the speaker on and there was a sound of rustling at the other end.

"I met with him," Peralta said, referring to the pimp. "Of course he wanted to know what was in it for him, but I didn't have to offer him much. I have a feeling he had a soft spot for the girl's mother, if that's possible for a pimp. In any case, he said she's dead."

"How did she die?" Colman asked.

"He said she was killed in a massacre that happened about two years ago. There were five people staying in a house, and a gang attacked them with machetes. They hacked them all to pieces, so we had trouble identifying the bodies."

"Why were they attacked?"

"They were working with a rival gang. Evidently the girl's mother got involved in drug distribution. Her pimp didn't know about it, and he wasn't happy when he found out. But he says he didn't kill her, and I believe him."

"Can you determine if she was one of the victims?"

"We have on record the DNA of a woman who was around her age. But we can't identify her unless we match it with the DNA of a close relative, and we don't know of any close relatives—except her daughter."

"When we find Marisol you can do a test," Gina said.

"At least we know," Colman said, "that whoever lured her to San Pedro lied about knowing where her mother was."

"Unless he was one of the guys who killed her," Peralta pointed out grimly.

"Is that likely?"

"No, it's not likely. But it's possible. The problem is, we don't know who killed her."

"So where does that leave us?"

"It leaves us with the trail from the airport," Peralta said, "and there we've made some progress. We found a driver who was there at the time the girl arrived, waiting to meet some people on her flight. And he remembers seeing a teenage girl being met by a guy who was holding a sign that said 'Mario.' We showed him her photo, and he made a positive identification."

"Thank God," Gina said with her heart going into second gear.

"It's a major break. But the driver had never seen the guy before, and he hasn't seen him since. All he remembers is that the guy was wearing a white linen suit and that he led the girl to a black Lincoln Town Car."

"That's what our limo services use," Colman said.

"Ours too. But the drivers don't wear white linen suits. So this guy probably owns the car, or he borrowed it, or he stole it."

"I assume that the driver you questioned didn't get a license number."

"No. He just saw the car, and then the people he was meeting arrived. Until we questioned him, he didn't think too much about it. The only thing that bothered him was why a man who could have been the girl's father would need to hold a sign for her."

"Are there a lot of Lincoln Town Cars here?" Gina asked.

"There're enough so it'll take us a while to check them all. But we're also checking at the hotels to see if anyone remembers seeing a man in a white linen suit with a teenage girl."

"Why would he take her to a hotel?" Colman asked. "He could be spotted there."

"He'd want to make her feel comfortable," Peralta said. "He'd want to make her trust him."

"And then what?"

"He'd take her where they could hold her captive."

Colman nodded, processing the information. "She arrived on Saturday. Could they still be at a hotel?"

"It depends on what he plans to do with her."

Not wanting to hear the options, Gina asked: "Well, what's he going to do when she asks him to take her to her mother?"

"He's going to stall," Peralta said. "He's going to make her feel that she has no choice but to trust him."

"But sooner or later he has to admit that he doesn't know where her mother is."

"He won't have to admit it until they have her under control."

"How would they get her under control?"

Peralta hesitated. "Just take my word for it. They have a lot of experience in turning children into slaves."

"Then we have to find them before that happens."

"I know we do. And I can't promise you that we will, but we'll do everything possible to find them. I can promise you that."

When the conversation ended, Gina silently repeated the prayer that had been running in her mind since the night Marisol went missing. "Blessed Mother, please protect her. Please don't let anything bad happen to her."

ELEVEN

THEY WERE ABOUT to go to lunch when Colman's phone rang. He answered in Spanish as if he thought it was Peralta calling, but it was Ron. Again he put his phone on speaker so that Gina could hear the other side of the conversation.

"Our geek found a piece of information that could be useful," Ron said. "It's a message on the girl's Facebook from a guy who called himself El Lobo."

"What did it say?" Colman asked.

"It said that if she gave him her phone number, he could tell her how to find the person she was looking for. He didn't use the word 'mother' or we would have found this message in our search using key words."

"Did she give him her phone number?"

"She did, but it was two weeks after his message. It looks like she had doubts about him."

"Were there any other messages from this guy?"

"No. That was the only one. So if he's the guy who lured her, then they communicated with text messages from that point on. And those messages would be on her phone."

"Can you tap into her phone?"

"No. We only have access to her Facebook."

"Well, we're still hoping to hear from her," Colman said, "but we're not counting on it."

"Yeah, I know," Ron said. "We'll keep searching, but I don't think we'll learn anything more from her Facebook."

During lunch, which they ate in the hotel restaurant, they talked about why Marisol might have been attracted by a guy who called himself El Lobo. The prospect of danger was suggested by the

162

name, and yet it may have seemed as unreal to her as the danger from the wolf to Red Riding Hood.

They were back in their room when the man at the desk called and told them a police officer was in the lobby waiting for them. As they rode down in the elevator they didn't talk because there were other people in the car, but they both knew what the other was feeling, and they held hands to comfort each other.

Peralta was at the desk, and without a word he beckoned them to go with him. When they got into the car that was stopped in front of the hotel, he broke his silence, saying: "We found the hotel where he took her. They're no longer there, but they left some things in the room, and we need you to identify them."

"How do you know they're not coming back?" Gina asked.

"We don't know, but it doesn't look like they are."

"When did they leave?" Colman asked.

"We think it was early this morning. Last night they had dinner at the hotel restaurant, and this morning when the maid came to clean the room they weren't there. She thought they'd gone out, and she didn't think too much about it until she went back later in the morning to replace a pillow, and then she found a note under it that said: 'Help.' "

"In English or in Spanish?" Gina asked.

"In English," Peralta said.

So the girl had finally found a use for the language that she had resisted.

The hotel wasn't far away, and it was in a higher price range than the hotel where they were staying. The guy had obviously wanted to impress Marisol.

When they got to the room they found two police officers searching it for clues.

It didn't take Gina long to spot Marisol's backpack on the floor and to find some clean underwear in a drawer.

"Are those hers?" Peralta asked gently.

"Yeah, they're hers. If they checked out, then why did she leave them?"

163

"They didn't check out. They just left. And of course he didn't pay the bill."

"But you must have a description of him," Colman said.

"We do, and we know who he is."

"Who is he?" Gina asked.

"He's a guy who works for one of the organizations that have taken over our country. He's no one important, but he has a record for petty theft and disorderly conduct."

"Do you know where you can find him?"

"We have some ideas, and the trail's fresh. They're probably still in the city because he left the car in the hotel garage. It was stolen," Peralta added.

"Why would they have suddenly left?" Colman asked.

"He might have learned that we were looking for them. Not from us, but from the people we were questioning at the hotels. They have a bigger network than we do."

At that moment a police officer approached Peralta with a plastic bag, saying: "We found this toothbrush in the bathroom."

"She didn't bring her toothbrush," Gina said.

"It must be a toothbrush that the hotel provided for guests," Peralta said, taking the bag from the officer.

"If she used it," Colman said, "you can get DNA from it."

"But she might not have used it," Gina said. "She doesn't brush her teeth regularly."

"We have that problem with our daughter too. Why don't they like to brush their teeth?"

"It's too much work. They can't be bothered. But please, dear God—" Gina was hoping that since Marisol had asked for help in English she might have brushed her teeth if only for the comfort in following a routine from home.

"If he learned that you were looking for them," Colman said, refocusing the conversation, "why didn't he take the car?"

"The car would be easier for us to spot," Peralta said. "If they're on foot, he can hide in the crowd."

"If they're on foot, then they're not going far."

"They're probably not. His organization probably has a location within walking distance."

"And you have men on the street watching for them."

"I have a man at every corner within two kilometers. But if she willingly goes with him," Peralta added, "they'll be harder for my men to spot."

"Why would she willingly go with him?"

"She would if she believes he's taking her to her mother."

"But she left that note under the pillow," Gina said, "so she's afraid of him."

"I know it sounds irrational," Peralta said, "but she could be afraid of him and still hope he'll take her to her mother."

"You mean her hope is stronger than her fear," Colman said.

"It usually is for most of us."

Something else had been bothering Gina, and suddenly she knew what it was. "Did you find her computer here?"

"No, we didn't. But we're not done searching the room."

"If her computer isn't here, then she didn't think they were coming back."

"How do you figure?"

"She wouldn't have left her computer here."

"But she left her underwear."

"That's not important. Her computer is the only thing that's important to her."

"Okay. You know her," Peralta said. "So if we don't find her computer here, we can conclude that she didn't think they were coming back."

"Well, if she left here hoping the guy would take her to her mother," Colman said, "when she realizes that he has something else in mind, she won't want to go with him."

"She won't be easy to deal with," Gina agreed.

"Then maybe she'll draw attention to them. Maybe someone will notice that she doesn't want to go with this guy. And maybe they'll call us."

Colman looked at her with an idea in his eyes which Gina understood, and she nodded in assent.

"We'll help you," he told Peralta. "Put us on a corner where we can watch for Marisol."

"You're serious?"

"Yes, we're serious. We don't want to sit around waiting to hear from you. We want to help you find her."

"Okay. I'll put you on a corner," Peralta said, accepting their offer. "I need all the help I can get."

They stayed until the police determined that Marisol hadn't left her computer, and then Peralta led them to a busy intersection, where they took a position in front of a restaurant and scanned the crowd of people, hoping to spot a man with a girl who was giving him a hard time.

Getting Marisol off the drugs was only a first step in the long process of raising a child. In fact, she had another addiction, which in some respects was worse than her addiction to the drugs. Ugo and Eileen had bought the computer for Marisol as a way of occupying her, just as they had bought a television set for the playroom downstairs as a way of putting her out of sight. And the girl was inseparable from the computer as if it was her security blanket. At home in Sudbury she took it to the dinner table, to the bathroom, and to bed at night.

When she came to live with Gina and Colman, they established some rules to limit her use of the computer: it wasn't allowed at the dinner table, and it wasn't allowed in bed at night. The first of these rules was less difficult to enforce, but the second rule led to a heated argument that ended with Marisol telling them she hated them and storming out of the house.

Gina went after her, caught up with her, told her they loved her, and persuaded her to come back after agreeing that the computer would be allowed in bed until ten o'clock. At that hour Gina went into Marisol's room, kissed her goodnight, and took the computer, which she placed for the night on top of the bureau in their bedroom.

Marisol complained that without the computer she couldn't sleep, so Gina suggested reading a book, but the girl said she didn't like to read. In fact, she had a reading deficiency that hadn't been identified by the school in Sudbury. It was revealed when Colman asked her to read aloud a story in the newspaper about the U.S. women's soccer team, which was expected to qualify for next year's World Cup. The way the girl read it, the story made no sense, and she had difficulty pronouncing any word that was more than two syllables.

From then on, before kissing Marisol goodnight Gina sat on her bed and read with her, doing a paragraph and having Marisol do the next paragraph, then alternating paragraphs until the girl's eyes began to droop. It wasn't as stimulating as the computer, but it helped Marisol go to sleep and it helped Gina bond with her.

At one of their meetings with Dr. Rivas they talked about the girl's addiction to her computer.

"She's not the only kid with that addiction," Dr. Rivas said. "We have a generation of kids who are addicted to their computers and their smartphones, and we don't know enough about the long-term effects. There are studies on the problem in South Korea, which was way ahead of us in wiring their society, but they don't provide any solutions."

"Could we use the same method we used for the drugs?" Gina asked. "I mean, could we gradually reduce the time she spends on her computer?"

"Sure. It sounds like you've already reduced the time."

"She still spends five or six hours a day on it."

"Well, instead of trying to reduce that time further, you could try to replace it with other activities."

"That makes sense," Colman said. "We need to help her find other things to do."

"If she had friends," Gina said, "she'd have other things to do. But with all the time she spends on her computer she doesn't have time to make friends, and since she doesn't have any friends she spends time on her computer. It's a vicious circle."

"She has to learn to make friends," Dr. Rivas said. "With her disorder she has trouble forming relationships with people."

"So how can we help her make friends?"

"You can get her involved in activities that give her opportunities to make friends."

"We got her involved in soccer, but she didn't make any friends from that."

"Those boys are very tough," Colman said. "They're not open to making friends, especially with girls. But now that Marisol's finally off the drugs, she can try out for the girls' soccer team at Sacred Heart."

"That's a good idea," Dr. Rivas said. "She'd be playing with girls who are schoolmates, and that could help her make friends with them."

"I keep thinking," Gina said, "that she'll make friends in the neighborhood. They're a lot of kids her age, and they all speak Spanish. And she does talk with the older people, but she avoids people her age."

"It's safer to talk with older people," Dr. Rivas said. "She has no risk of being rejected."

After a silence Colman said: "I have this feeling that something terrible happened to her before she went to the orphanage. Do you have any idea what it was?"

Dr. Rivas shook her head. "Marisol says she doesn't remember anything that happened before she went there. It's probably true. I mean, if anything did happen, she's repressed it. And in her present situation I think the cost would outweigh the benefit of digging it up."

"I assume you talk with Susan about her," Gina said.

"We talk about her every two weeks. And we agree on not digging up her past now. But we do know that something terrible happened to her."

"We do? What?" Colman asked.

"She was abandoned by her birth mother."

"I have trouble understanding what that did to her."

"I do too. With all my studies and all my experience, I still have trouble understanding what it did to her. I only understand that it impedes her process of forming attachments."

"Do you think she has an attachment to us?" Gina asked.

"I think she does."

"I don't feel it."

"You don't have to feel it," Dr. Rivas said. "It's there. But I assume you're not looking for reciprocity."

"I'm not, though it would be nice to feel love in return."

Dr. Rivas nodded. "It's hard for us to love unconditionally. But we must try to love children that way."

"I know, and we're trying."

"So keep trying. This child has a good heart, and eventually I think you'll reach it."

Marisol made the girls' soccer team, and she was on the starting roster. They played thirteen games, and they won most of them. They practiced regularly together, and at least Marisol knew the names of all her teammates. But she didn't develop relationships with any of them. She didn't hang out with them, and she didn't have a sleepover with any of them. She kept retreating from the real world and going into the virtual world.

From conversations with the doctor and the therapist, Gina understood that a major obstacle to Marisol's ability to form relationships with her classmates was that she was emotionally young for her age, so she wasn't at the same stage of development as her peers. The girls her age were interested in boys, and the boys her age were interested in girls, but she hadn't reached this stage of development, or at least she didn't show it. Whatever was going on with her in the realm of sexuality, she didn't reveal it, even to Dr. Rivas, with whom she could have talked about it in Spanish. But as the doctor suggested, maybe not much was going on because emotionally Marisol was still at the stage of pre-adolescence.

Since she had no experience in raising children, Gina had no comparative expectations for Marisol's behaviors, which left her open and nonjudgmental, but also left her wondering if these behaviors were within a wide range of normality. For information she went to Leonora, who had raised two girls, and she asked Leonora when her girls started taking showers willingly. When they started changing their underwear daily. When they started noticing cute boys. When they started worrying about their hair and skin. When they started caring about the clothes they wore. When they started knowing the words to songs they heard on the radio. The answers supported the doctor's opinion that Marisol wasn't behaving like most teenage girls, which Leonora said should be counted as a blessing.

One set of Marisol's behaviors that concerned Gina had to do with food. From her experience Gina understood that children tended to resist the expansion of their diets from items they trusted to new items. In her own family, which had traditional Italian dinners at the table with children expected to eat what the grownups ate, her brother refused to eat vegetables, displaying a veritable phobia of anything green, and unlike Gina and Leonora, who at the time weren't keen on vegetables, Ugo was allowed a dispensation from them. Years later, as a father of four children, he still made a fuss if anything green was passed his way at the dinner table, acting as if people were trying to poison him with green beans, green peas, or green leafy vegetables. Evidently taking her cue from him, Marisol refused to eat anything green, including parsley which restaurants often sprinkled over dishes for esthetic purposes. Once when they were eating in an Italian restaurant on Main Street, where they went often because it was close, the food was good, and the prices were reasonable, the chef, who should have known better by now, sprinkled parsley on Marisol's ravioli, and in her own way she made a scene, not as Ugo would have by yelling and screaming and stamping his feet, but by silently picking each fleck of parsley off her ravioli before she would touch it. The waiter, seeing the girl's distress, offered to replace the dish with uncontaminated ravioli, but Marisol shook her head and glumly continued to remove the offending flecks of green.

It wasn't only green vegetables that Marisol refused to eat, it was virtually everything except pasta, soda, and cookies. From what Gina had seen at the house in Sudbury, the typical dinner was lasagna or some other pasta from Stew Leonard's that Eileen only had to warm up in the microwave. Of course Eileen had a job outside the home, which in her mind justified not cooking, but she didn't seem to know that pasta was only a part of an Italian meal, it wasn't the whole meal, and it wasn't something people lived on unless they had nothing else to eat. But Eileen's family, who resided in one of the most affluent towns in the nation, lived on pasta as if they were peasants in an Italy that only existed in the minds of ignorant Americans.

Then there was the soda. At the house in Sudbury they drank a case of soda every day, following the example of Eileen, who drank Coca Cola for breakfast, lunch, and dinner every day, so when Marisol came to live in Yonkers she was used to drinking soda that was laced with caffeine and loaded with sugar. In a process that mirrored getting her off the psychiatric medication, Gina took the girl from Coca Cola to non-caffeinated soda and finally to water, which they got through a filter on the faucet of the sink.

And then the cookies. At the house in Sudbury they ate dozens of cookies every day, following the example of Ugo, who ate a box of cookies every night with a glass of milk, so when Marisol came to live in Yonkers she was used to eating cookies that were sold in boxes or bags. The store-bought cookies were replaced with home-made biscotti, which weren't available as a daily snack but only as an occasional treat.

So Gina and Colman were able to make some adjustments that they believed would improve the girl's health, but whenever they began to feel they were making some progress with her behavior, they had a setback.

One such setback occurred during the spring of Marisol's sophomore year. About once a week Gina stopped at the cash machine on Main Street and withdrew a hundred dollars in twenties, which she kept in a wallet inside her pocketbook. When she was at home she left her pocketbook on top of the bureau in their bedroom, and one day when she checked her cash before going out she found that she had twenty dollars less than she thought she had. Of course she could have forgotten where she had spent that twenty, so she didn't jump to any conclusion, but she did start keeping track of how much money was in her wallet, and a week later she found that there was twenty dollars missing. Just to make sure, she asked Colman if he had taken it, and when he said he hadn't she knew that Marisol had taken it. She was reluctant to confront Marisol, knowing how vulnerable she was, but after discussing the matter with Colman she finally went to the girl's room, where she found her sprawled on the bed with her computer.

"We need to talk," she told Marisol.

"Okay," the girl said, engrossed in the screen.

"I want your attention, so please stop whatever you're doing."

"I can talk and do this at the same time."

"No, you can't. Please look at me."

Marisol looked up from her computer as if she was annoyed by the interruption. "Okay. I'm looking at you."

"There's twenty dollars missing from my wallet. Did you take it?"

"No," Marisol said, shaking her head vigorously.

"Are you sure?"

"I'm sure."

"Well, someone took it," Gina said, "and it wasn't Colman."

"Maybe it's not missing. Maybe you forgot that you spent it on something."

"No. I know how much money was in my wallet."

"I didn't take it," Marisol cried with tears in her eyes.

Though Gina knew she had taken it, she felt bad about accusing her. "If you need money, you should ask for it. I'll give it to you."

"I didn't take it," Marisol screamed.

"Okay," Gina said, understanding why the girl couldn't admit that she had done something wrong. She put her arms around Marisol and said: "I love you, and I'll always love you, no matter what happens. So don't be afraid to tell the truth."

Marisol only allowed the hug, and she said nothing.

That evening, after Marisol had gone up to her room, Gina and Colman talked about what had happened. They agreed that since the girl was so vulnerable, they had to be gentle with her, and they had to be flexible regarding her behavior, but when she did something wrong they had to draw a line, and they had to make her understand the difference between right and wrong. They agreed that Colman would go upstairs and impress on her that stealing was wrong, that they expected her never to steal again, and that they had already forgiven her.

When he returned, Colman said: "She admitted it, and she promised never to do it again."

"Thank God. You talked with her in Spanish?"

"Yeah. I think she feels less vulnerable in Spanish."

"I can understand that. Whenever I talked with my mother about a personal problem, it was in Italian."

Colman sat down at the kitchen table, where she was sitting. "I asked her why she needed money, and she said it was to buy soda and cookies."

"I thought we got her off that junk."

"Evidently she still has a craving for it now and then. And she was afraid to ask us to buy it, or to ask us for money to buy it."

Gina sighed. "That makes me feel bad. I mean, we did it for her own good. But I don't want her to be afraid of us."

"I don't think she's generally afraid of us. I think it was just in that situation."

"Well, I've been giving her an allowance of ten dollars a week. Should I give her more?"

"Maybe," Colman said. "But maybe it would be better if she had her own money."

"She could earn money by babysitting."

"You think she'd be good at that?"

"I think she would be. She has no problem relating to children who are younger. She only has a problem with people her age."

"So let's look for opportunities."

"I'll ask Kenia. With her new baby, she could use some help with her other two kids."

Kenia, who lived two doors down the block, said she could definitely use some help, and when Gina relayed this information to Marisol, the girl responded positively. In fact, she knew the names of the older kids, who were two and four.

Marisol sat with the kids for three hours, twice a week, which gave Kenia time for her baby. Kenia told Gina that Marisol was wonderful with her children, and that she would be happy to recommend her to everyone in the neighborhood. Gina relayed this compliment to Marisol, hoping it would help her build a core of self-worth. As a tiny green shoot, she noticed that Marisol looked pleased by the compliment.

The job not only gave Marisol some money of her own, it also got her away from her computer for six hours a week, in line with the policy of replacing time on the computer with time in the real world. But it didn't give her an opportunity to make friends with people her age, so as soon as she returned from Kenia's she went back into the virtual world.

Colman's phone suddenly rang. It was Peralta, and moving closer to the front of the restaurant, Colman put the phone on speaker.

"We found her," Peralta said. "She's all right. But she has some bruises and a broken arm, so she's in the hospital."

"How do we get there?" Colman asked.

"You can take a taxi. I'm at the station now copying messages from her phone."

"Did you catch him?"

"No. But we have him cornered."

"How did she get the bruises and the broken arm?" Gina asked, though she could easily imagine.

"He beat her up. He was trying to make her go into a building, and she resisted. They were out on the street, where people could see them. And someone actually called the police."

"So he left her on the street?"

"Yeah. A crowd was gathering around them, and he must have realized that he wasn't in a good situation because he was gone before my men got there."

"What's the name of the hospital?"

Peralta told them, and then he said: "For some reason, he took her computer. Maybe he thought there was evidence on it, but all the evidence is on her phone. It has all the messages they exchanged."

"Except for his message on Facebook," Colman pointed out.

"Well, that's all he'll find on her computer."

When the call had ended Gina and Colman hugged each other and thanked God for rescuing their goddaughter. People walking by them paused to stare and even smile, heartened by their good fortune, whatever it was.

Without delay they headed toward the street, where they could hail a taxi.

TWELVE

WITH ALL THE traffic, it took them more than a half hour to get to the hospital, and it took another half hour to find out that Marisol was in an operating room having surgery on her arm. So they sat in a waiting area for almost two hours before they could see her.

She was sharing a room with a girl who according to the nurse had been wounded by a gunshot. The girl was dozing, and Marisol was still recovering from the anesthetic they had given her, so she was groggy and confused.

"Where am I?" she asked.

"You're in a hospital," Gina said.

"In Yonkers?"

"No. In San Pedro Sula."

"How did I get here?"

"We'll tell you soon enough, but you should try to rest now."

Marisol looked down at her plaster cast. "What happened to my arm?"

"It was broken in a fight you had with a guy."

"What guy?"

"The guy who lured you here."

Marisol blinked her eyes as if she was trying to clear the cobwebs from her brain. Then suddenly she asked: "Where's my computer?"

"He took it," Gina said.

"He took my computer?" Marisol said, alarmed.

"The police are trying to get it back," Colman assured her. "But if they don't get it back, we'll buy you another computer."

"I don't want another computer. My whole life is on that computer."

"Your real life isn't on that computer," Gina said. "Only your virtual life is on it."

Marisol shook her head, not in denial but in disbelief.

At that moment Peralta came into the room.

Colman introduced him to Marisol and explained that he was the man who had rescued her.

"Rescued me from what?"

"From being hurt much more than you were," Gina said.

"The doctor said your arm will be fine," Peralta told Marisol. "He noticed that the same arm had been broken before. How did that happen?"

"It happened in a soccer match," Marisol said. "Did you get back my computer?"

"We're trying to get it back. I know how important it is, but your arm is more important. Trust me."

Marisol looked at Peralta as if she might consider trusting him, but then she asked: "What about my phone?"

"I have your phone. I need to keep it for a while as evidence against the guy who beat you up, but then I'll give it back to you."

"Okay," Marisol said, beginning to fade.

"You should try to rest now," Gina said, laying her hand on Marisol's shoulder. "We'll stay here with you. We won't go anywhere until they're ready to check you out."

"The doctor said they'll want to keep her here for the night," Peralta said. "She suffered some heavy blows to the head, so they want to monitor her."

"Can we stay here all night?"

"Oh, yes. They expect members of the family to help the nurses take care of patients."

They waited until Marisol was asleep, and then with Peralta they left the room.

In the hallway he said: "I have her phone with me. We copied the messages she exchanged with El Lobo so we have the evidence. But I thought you should look at those messages. They might help you understand what happened."

"Do you want us to return her phone to you?" Colman asked.

"No, you can give it to her. We have its serial number, we have a photo of it, and we have a transcript of the messages."

"I gather you haven't caught him yet."

"We have him trapped in a building with other members of his gang. We've given them an ultimatum, so it's only a matter of time now before they surrender."

"Well, I hope no one gets hurt," Gina said, "especially none of your officers."

"We're getting better at not getting hurt," Peralta said.

He handed her the phone, and then he left them.

They found a waiting area where they could sit next to each other and look at the messages in Marisol's phone. They were all in Spanish, so at times Colman had to translate for her.

It had started toward the end of March with a message from El Lobo that said: "You said on your Facebook that you were born in San Pedro Sula. Is that true?"

"Yes, it's true," Marisol responded.

"How old are you?"

"I'm eighteen."

"Where do you live now?"

Marisol didn't respond to that message. Evidently she had enough sense not to tell her virtual friends where she lived.

A few days later El Lobo texted: "You said you were adopted and taken to the United States. Is that true?"

"Yes, it's true."

"How long ago did that happen?"

"Eleven years ago."

"So you were seven when you were adopted?"

"Yes," Marisol responded.

"Where did you live before?"

"In an orphanage."

"When was the last time you saw your mother?"

"I'm not sure. I think it was about thirteen years ago."

"Do you have a photo of your mother?"

"No. I wish I did, but I don't."

"Do you remember what she looked like?"

"I have an image of her in my mind."

"You said you wanted to find her," El Lobo texted.

"I do. But I don't know where to look for her."

"Well, if you give me the name of the orphanage, I can help you find her."

"I don't know the name of the orphanage, but I'll find out."

Reading this message, Gina wondered how Marisol expected to find out the name of the orphanage. She didn't remember the girl saying anything about it

After a few days Marisol texted: "I couldn't find out the name of the orphanage."

"All right," El Lobo replied. "I'll find out for you."

"Thanks. I really appreciate it."

Two weeks passed without any messages, and then El Lobo texted: "I found your mother."

"You did? Where is she?"

"She's in San Pedro."

"Where exactly in San Pedro?"

"If you come here, I'll take you to her."

"Are you in San Pedro?"

"Yes. I live here."

A few days later Marisol texted: "If you tell me where my mother is, I can find her myself."

"That would be dangerous."

"Why would it be dangerous?"

"San Pedro is a dangerous place."

"If it is, then why do you live there?"

"I was born here. I have no choice."

A week later Marisol texted: "Do you want money for taking me to my mother?"

"Of course I want money for helping you."

"How much do you want?"

"Five hundred dollars."

"Well, if I pay you five hundred dollars, how do I know you'll take me to my mother?"

"You don't have to pay me until I take you to her."

Several days later Marisol texted: "I want to go to San Pedro. How can I get there?"

"You can take a direct flight from Miami."

"Am I old enough to fly by myself?"

"Yes. You're eighteen."

The next day Marisol texted: "I checked the airline schedules, and I could be on a flight that arrives in San Pedro Sula at 1:30 on Saturday, May 31."

"That would be perfect. I'll meet you at the airport."

"How will I know you? You don't have a photo on Facebook."

"I'll have a sign with your name on it."

Two days passed, and then Marisol texted: "I should tell you now so you won't be surprised. I'm not a boy, I'm a girl."

"I knew that," El Lobo responded.

"How did you know that?"

"When I tracked down your mother, I learned that she had only one child, and it was a girl."

"Do you know my real name?"

"No. I didn't see your birth certificate."

"Then you can still call me Mario."

"Why not María?"

"I don't like that name."

"Okay. I'll still call you Mario, and that's the name I'll put on the sign."

On Friday, May 30 Marisol texted: "I'll be on the flight from Miami tomorrow. Please confirm that you'll be at the airport."

"I'll be at the airport," El Lobo responded.

After reading the messages Gina and Colman sat back in silence, processing what they had learned about their goddaughter.

Colman was the first to break the silence, saying: "She knew she was taking a risk."

"She did. And she had doubts," Gina added.

"Yeah, she kept stopping and thinking about the next step."

"But then she kept going ahead."

"The guy was clever," Colman said after a pause. "I mean, the way he used her revelation that she was a girl, not a boy. He pretended he learned it from tracking down her mother, and that gave him credibility."

"Yeah, he even had a good explanation for not knowing her real name."

"So we were on the wrong track when we wondered what he'd do when he found out that she was a girl. He already knew that, and he already had plans to use her as a girl."

Gina reflected. "I wonder when she realized that he wasn't taking her to her mother."

"It must have been when he tried to make her go into that building, though it could have been sooner. Maybe that's why she took her computer when they left the hotel—so she'd have it with her if she ran away."

"As she said, her whole life is on that computer."

"What I don't understand is why she suddenly needed to find her birth mother."

"She might have just reached a turning point. I mean, she was eighteen, she was graduating from high school, and she was about to move on to the next stage of her life. So maybe she had to know her past before she could deal with her future."

"Maybe," Colman said. "I don't remember anything that might have set her off, do you?"

"No. She had a need, and that guy detected it."

"He detected it, and he exploited it."

"But if we'd satisfied her need," Gina said, feeling the weight of failure, "he wouldn't have been able to exploit it."

"Remember, Dr. Rivas said there's a void in her that can never be filled completely."

"I remember, but I feel we should have been able to fill it."

"She warned us that we wouldn't be able to fill it."

"That shouldn't have stopped us from trying to fill it, and it shouldn't stop us now."

"We'll keep trying," Colman said, taking her hand.

Before going to see how Marisol was doing, Colman called Ron and told him they had found their goddaughter. Gina couldn't hear Ron's exact words, but from his whoop of joy she could tell how he felt. And speaking into the phone she added her thanks to Colman's for all the help that Ron had given them.

In the room they found Marisol sitting up in bed, awake. She no longer looked confused, but she didn't look alert.

"How are you feeling?" Gina asked her, standing by the bed.

"I don't know," Marisol said, shrugging.

"Do you have a headache?"

"A little, but my arm hurts more."

"Do you remember how your arm got broken?" Colman asked, sitting on the edge of the bed.

"Yeah, it was that guy. He was trying to make me go into a building, and when I refused, he grabbed my arm and twisted it. He threw me down, and I landed on it."

"Why did you refuse to go into the building?"

"I had a feeling he was going to kill me."

"Why would he have killed you?"

"I don't know. I don't understand what he wanted from me."

"Did you ever pay him the five hundred dollars?"

Looking surprised, Marisol asked "How do you know about the money?"

"We read the messages on your phone," Gina told her.

"Then you know the whole story?"

"We know how he lured you here, but we don't know why you believed he was taking you to your mother."

"I don't know why. I guess I wanted to believe him, and—" Marisol looked accusingly from one of them to the other. "There was no one else I could believe."

"What do you mean?"

"I mean, I knew my parents were lying about what happened to my mother. And I knew why they were lying. They didn't want me to find my mother."

"What about us?" Gina asked, ready to take the consequences of her question.

"You were lying too. You said she died in a car accident."

"That's what your parents told us."

"Well, you shouldn't have believed them."

"You mean we should have known they were lying?"

"Yeah, you should have known. They lie about everything."

"Okay. We're sorry," Gina said, speaking for both of them. "But we only found out a few days ago that they were lying about your mother."

Marisol's eyes brightened a little. "So she wasn't killed in a car accident?"

"No, she wasn't, though she might have been killed another way. We're waiting to hear from Inspector Peralta."

"Then I might not ever see her?"

"You might not," Gina said, gently laying a hand on Marisol's shoulder.

Tears started flowing from Marisol's eyes. "If I don't ever see her, then how will I know what she was like? And how will I ever know who I am?"

"There are people who can tell you what she was like," Colman said. "But no one can tell you who you are."

"Or who you should be," Gina said.

After a silence Marisol said: "Well, I know who I'm not. I'm not Meredith."

"That's a start. And you have your whole life to keep learning."

At that point a woman rolled a cart into the room. It had bottles of juice and a plate of food that looked like tamales.

"Are you hungry?" Gina asked.

"No, but I'm thirsty. What kind of juices do you have?" Marisol asked the woman.

"Orange, pineapple, and mango," the woman said.

"I'll have mango, please."

Marisol was drinking the mango juice when Peralta appeared with a carrying case. "Guess what we found."

"You found my computer?" Marisol said, her eyes lighting up.

"We arrested the guy, and he had it with him."

Remembering how Marisol had said that her whole life was on that computer, Gina wondered if finding it might not have been the next best thing to finding her mother, at least for the purpose of knowing who she was. And with more empathy than she would have felt only a week ago, she watched Marisol receive the carrying case, open it, take out the computer, and press the button to turn it on. "The battery's dead. Where's the charger?"

"Wherever you left it," Peralta said, sounding like a typical parent.

"Oh, my God. I left it in the hotel room."

"Yes, you did. And we found it there." Out of a side pocket of his jacket Peralta took the charger with its coiled cord, and he handed it to Marisol.

"*Gracias*," she said.

"*De nada*," he said with a slight bow.

After Colman plugged in the charger for her, Marisol started her computer and immediately became engrossed in it. In that sense nothing had changed.

"Could we step outside and talk for a moment?" Peralta asked them in a low voice.

"Yeah, sure," Gina said, guessing what he wanted to tell them.

Out in the hallway Peralta said: "We completed the DNA analysis. The woman who was killed in that massacre was Marisol's mother."

Gina sighed with a mixture of sorrow and relief.

"I thought she should learn that from you, not from me."

"I agree," Colman said. "I just don't know when we should tell her. What do you think?"

"I think we should wait and give her time to process our last conversation," Gina said. "And right now she has her computer, which is occupying her mind."

"They really love their electronic toys," Peralta said. "My daughter would have reacted the same way."

"Speaking of your daughter," Colman said. "We owe you more than words can say, and I'll do everything I can to bring her to America—with her family."

"I only asked you to bring *her* there," Peralta said.

"But she needs her family," Gina said.

"Well, it would be better for her to go there without her family than to stay here with her family and get killed."

"That's why we have to bring her family there," Colman said. "We could start with her and bring you later."

"She could live with us until you get there," Gina offered.

"You mean you want to take on another teenage girl?"

"Why not? It would be good for Marisol to have a younger sister. And it would only be until Colman gets you and her mother into our country."

"If she was already there as a refugee," Colman said, "then we'd have a legal argument for bringing you and her mother in. Our government is making things harder for immigrants, but we have a strong moral tradition of keeping families together."

Peralta nodded solemnly. "Okay. I'll talk with my wife and get back to you."

They exchanged abrazos, and Peralta left.

Returning to the room, they found Marisol totally involved with her computer, and they had trouble getting her attention.

"We're going to spend the night here," Gina said. "I don't know where, but we'll find a place. So we'll be around if you need us. Okay?"

"Okay," Marisol said without looking up from the screen.

At lights-out time the nurse made Marisol turn off her computer and lie down. After kissing her goodnight Gina spent the night sitting in a chair by the bed while Colman found a quiet place in a waiting area. Neither of them slept much, but Marisol fell into a deep sleep and didn't stir until the morning shift came on and woke up the patients.

Shortly after ten the next morning they got Marisol released from the hospital. Since she wasn't covered by Eileen's health insurance in a foreign country, Colman charged the bill to his credit card, pointing out how much more the hospital's services would have cost at home.

They took Marisol back to their hotel, and they had lunch in the hotel restaurant, where by now the waitstaff knew them.

Colman booked flights for the next day, and they spent the rest of the day taking a guided tour of the city. The sights included the cathedral, where they each lit a candle to thank God for rescuing Marisol, the central park, the museum of archeology, the crafts market, and Angeli Gardens with its wonderful view. They agreed that the city was an interesting place to visit, but since it had such a high murder rate, they didn't want to live there.

While they were resting in their room before dinner, Gina decided that it would be a good time to tell Marisol the truth about her mother. Marisol was lying next to her on the bed they would share that night, and Colman was lying on the other bed.

"We found out what happened to your mother," Gina told Marisol. "The police confirmed that she was killed about two years ago in a gang massacre."

"My mother was a member of a gang?"

"She was working with a gang."

"What was she doing with them?"

"Distributing drugs."

"How did they kill her?"

"You really want to know?"

"Yeah. I really want to know."

"They killed her with machetes."

There was a gurgling sound as if Marisol was suppressing an urge to throw up.

"That's why they couldn't identify her until yesterday."

"What happened yesterday?"

"They matched DNA samples from her and you."

"Where did they get a sample from me?"

"From the toothbrush you left in the hotel room where that guy took you."

Marisol made a face of disgust as if she was remembering things that had happened in the hotel room. "Well, just so you know, I didn't let him touch me."

"Did he try to touch you?"

"Not exactly, but I had a feeling he wanted to. It was really creepy," Marisol said, making a face.

"I can imagine," Gina said. "But you don't have to worry about him. They'll put him away for at least ten years."

"He might not survive that long in prison," Colman added.

After a silence Marisol asked: "Was my mother a *puta*?"

"She sold her body for sex," Gina said.

"Then I was an accident, and my father must have been a guy who paid to have sex with her."

"I think it's likely."

"When did she take me to the orphanage?"

"She didn't take you there. You were found on the street, abandoned by her."

"How old was I then?"

"You were three years old."

"So she didn't even *take* me to the orphanage. She left me on the street, where anything could have happened to me."

"Well, luckily nothing did happen to you."

"How do you know?"

"There's no evidence that anything happened to you," Colman said, "while you were on the street."

"But she just left me there."

"She visited you once at the orphanage," Gina said. "I don't know how she knew you were there, but she must have made an effort to find you."

"I remember a woman visiting me," Marisol said in a faraway voice. "I thought she might have been my mother, but she never came back."

"A sister at the orphanage referred her to a lay worker who helps women get off the street. But she didn't stay off the street for long. And then she got involved with a gang."

After another silence Marisol said: "Well, I'm glad I didn't find her. I'm glad she's dead."

"She must have had a miserable life," Gina said, "and she died horribly. So you should have some compassion for her."

"Maybe when I'm older I will, but not now."

At that point Colman got up and sat down on the edge of their bed, saying: "Could you help us understand why you wanted to find your birth mother?"

"I thought if I found her," Marisol said, "she'd love me."

"I understand. But there's something you need to know," Gina said, hoping for a breakthrough. "Unlike your birth mother, I didn't get pregnant and have a baby I didn't want. And unlike your adoptive mother, I didn't take you and then decide you weren't what I wanted. When I took you, I knew what you were, and you were what I wanted. I loved you then, I love you now, and I'll love you always, no matter what happens."

With tears in her eyes Marisol took Gina's hand, saying: "I know, mom. I know."

Colman joined his hand to theirs, and together they made a family pact.

BOOK CLUB GUIDE

The Godmother

Tom Milton

Introduction

Gina Moretti begins to worry when her goddaughter, Marisol, doesn't come home from work at the usual time and doesn't respond to text messages. There is evidence in Marisol's room that she plans to stay overnight with someone, and since she has no friends from school or from the neighborhood, she might have gone to stay with someone she met on the internet. But the girl has taken her laptop and her smartphone with her, leaving no trail. The only clue emerges from her history. When she was almost seven Marisol was adopted from an orphanage in Honduras by Gina's brother and sister-in-law, who at the time thought they couldn't have children. After they had three children of their own they decided they couldn't handle Marisol, and they turned her over to Gina and her husband, who had a long relationship with her because she had spent weekends with them from the time she was adopted. Over the past four years they have given her a parental love that she never experienced before, but on the eve of her graduation from high school, she disappears. With the help of the local police, they learn that Marisol has evidently gone to meet someone in Honduras who claims to know where her birth mother is, so they follow her trail to the city with the highest murder rate in the world.

While following the trail of her goddaughter, Gina retraces the family history that brought her to the present situation, beginning with her grandparents, who immigrated from Italy and established themselves in a corner of the Bronx. They had six children, with five girls before they had a boy, Gianni, who grew up expecting women to serve him. When he finally got married, it was to a woman who devoted her life to him and their children. Gina was their first child, and she was followed by Leonora before Ugo appeared on the scene, repeating family history because he was the only boy in his generation. After years of working as a salesperson for a company that made equipment for home kitchens, Gianni started his own kitchen business in Manhattan, which struggled at first and prevented Gina from going to college because her family needed the income she could earn from working. When the business finally was successful, Gianni spent the profits on a mansion in Yonkers, trips to Italy, and parties, culminating in a bash at the grand ballroom of the Waldorf-Astoria.

By the time Gina could reconsider going to college, her mother had cancer, and the family was strapped with medical expenses because Gianni had no health insurance. Before dying, her mother made Gina promise to take care of her father, which she dutifully did. Her responsibilities included Ugo, whom she helped to complete a degree in computer engineering. She was still living with her father when Ugo got married and bought a house in Sudbury, Connecticut, with a loan from Gianni to finance the down payment. With his son settled, Gianni decided to sell the business and retire. He got the price he wanted for the business but only by accepting notes from the buyers for most of the payment. With the upfront money, he went to Italy for a year, and when he returned, the business was failing because the buyers had sold the inventory without replacing it and had bailed out, defaulting on the notes and letting ownership of the business revert to him. Appealing to her family loyalty, he persuaded Gina to give up her promising career with a large international printing company and to assume responsibility for running the business. Since she was a competent manager, she was able to turn the business around, but she didn't get any help from her father, who by then was pursuing his dream of becoming another Frank Sinatra, going daily to the senior center in the Bronx neighborhood where he grew up and entertaining his generation with songs that reminded them of their youth.

For the next five years Gina committed herself to the family business, supporting her father and providing financial assistance to her brother. Meanwhile, her brother and his wife had adopted Marisol, and Gina had become her godmother, a role whose responsibilities she took very seriously. She tried to protect Marisol from the efforts of her adoptive parents to make her fit what they wanted in a child, beginning with a change in her name from Marisol to Meredith, but they had ultimate authority over the child, so Gina was unable to prevent them from damaging her further. Disappointed in his son for not providing a male heir,

Gianni gave up on life and died, leaving Gina to deal with his legacy. Realizing that the family-owned business couldn't compete with the chain stores that sold kitchen equipment, she liquidated it, and seeing no point in keeping the mansion where she was now living alone, she sold it and moved into an apartment. Free from her family responsibilities, she developed a relationship with Colman, the lawyer who handled the closing for the mansion, and within a year she married him and moved into his house in a Latino neighborhood of Yonkers, where he served the local community and helped kids who got into trouble. Based on her experience, she got a job as a manager at a high-end kitchen store in Yonkers, which paid her well and gave her a lot of satisfaction. She was forty-seven, too old to have her own children, so she continued to fulfill her role as a godmother.

When her brother and his wife had three children of their own who fit what they wanted, they no longer had a reason for having Marisol, and they let Gina and Colman have her, instead of putting her in a foster home. Gina and Colman tried very hard to undo the damage done to Marisol from first being abandoned by her birth mother and then being abandoned by her adoptive mother, believing that their love could help her build a core of self-worth. When she suddenly leaves them to find her birth mother, they feel she has rejected their love, but they continue to pursue their mission of trying to save her, this time from a world that would turn her into a sex slave or a drug mule.

A conversation with Tom Milton

In each of your novels, while you tell a good story with believable characters, you also address a social issue, and I think this novel is mainly about what happens to children when they're not loved.

That's right. When they're not accepted for what they are.

You preface this novel with a quotation from Thomas Merton, who says that the beginning of love is to let those we love be perfectly themselves, and not to twist them to fit our own image. I can see how this idea applies to what her adoptive parents did to Marisol. They twisted her to fit their own image, beginning with the change of her name from Marisol to Meredith.

They tried to make her what they wanted, instead of letting her be herself.

What they wanted was a white baby whose parents had no vices and no health problems, and what they got was a brown girl who was almost seven at the time of adoption, whose mother was a prostitute and a drug addict, so she was a real challenge for them.

She certainly was, but they had options on how to deal with the challenge. For one thing, she had a lot of hidden anger, but instead of letting her channel that anger into a structured activity like soccer, they removed her from sports and put her on drugs to make her easier to manage.

Well, that's a problem in our society—the extent to which children are put on drugs to make them easier to manage.

I'm not faulting parents in general or teachers in general or doctors in general, but I *am* faulting those parents, teachers, or doctors who are looking for an easy way to deal with children. Drugs may be helpful in some cases, but they're being used far too broadly, and even when they *are* helpful, they only deal with the symptoms of a problem.

Let's talk about this girl's problem. She was born in Honduras, she was abandoned by her birth mother before she was three, she was consigned to an orphanage for several years, she was adopted by an American couple when she was almost seven, she was abandoned by her adoptive parents when she was fourteen, and she's diagnosed with reactive attachment disorder, which basically means she has trouble forming relationships with people.

There are a lot of children like her, who in one way or another have been abandoned by their mothers, and that leaves them permanently damaged.

There's no way of repairing that damage?

There's no way of undoing it. But there are ways of enabling these children to rise above the ashes of their early lives.

That's what Gina believes. I must say, I like it that Gina is the child's godmother, not a foster mother. It tells us something about how Gina sees her responsibilities toward this child.

As a godmother, she has responsibilities, but she doesn't have prerogatives. She can love her godchildren without hope that her life will be enhanced by their successes and without fear that it will be ruined by their failures.

That kind of love makes her free to let Marisol be herself.

At least it makes her free to put the needs of her goddaughter ahead of her own needs.

Through the flashbacks we learn that Gina has always put the needs of her family ahead of her own needs, to a point where she has missed out on some things in life.

She has, but she continues to pursue her mission, which is her family.

So her life is determined by her family?

I think all our lives are determined by our families, though the lives of some members are more determined by their family than the lives of other members. For example, we all know families in which one of the children takes responsibility for aging parents while the others have a free ride.

I can relate to that situation. Like Gina, I come from an Italian family, and I was the one who was designated to take responsibility for our aging parents.

Who designated you?

My mother. Though unlike Gina's mother, she didn't make me promise anything, I knew what she expected me to do. But let's not talk about my family. There's another problem I want to talk about.

What problem?

The problem of addiction to the internet. Marisol's adoptive parents got her addicted not only to drugs but also to the internet through her computer and her smartphone.

Like so many parents, they gave her those toys to keep her occupied, so they didn't have to pay attention to her.

You think it's a serious problem?

I think it's a very serious problem. I have students who are Marisol's age, and when they're on their smartphones, it breaks my heart to see them looking for shots of dopamine to make them feel good about themselves, especially because it often has the opposite effect.

What do you mean?

There are studies that show a relationship between the use of smartphones and teenage depression. In other words, the more time they spend on their smartphones, the greater their symptoms of depression.

You mean the smartphones cause depression?

That's still being debated. Defenders of smartphones explain the relationship by arguing that kids who already suffer from depression spend more time on the internet to escape from their feelings, but even in those cases, the internet makes them feel worse because they see other kids their age who have everything going for them.

You mean they see kids who pretend *to have everything going for them.*

In the virtual world, you can't tell if they're pretending. There's no reality check.

So do you believe the internet causes depression?

I believe it causes a lot of problems, and when the kids already have problems, it makes them worse. If they're already depressed, it makes them feel worse.

But if it makes Marisol feel worse, then why is she attracted to the internet?

It validates her negative feelings about herself.

Why would she want to have them validated?

They're all she has.

Okay. She believes what people say on the internet, and when someone comes along who pretends to know where her birth mother is, she believes him. But what does she hope to find with her birth mother?

She hopes to find love.

She already has love from her godmother and from her uncle.

She doesn't know she already has it. Since she didn't get love at the age when you learn what it is, she has trouble recognizing it.

You mean she has trouble recognizing the kind of love that Thomas Merton was talking about.

Right. The kind of love that will let her be perfectly herself.

Discussion questions

1. What is the main theme of this novel? What are some of the other themes?

2. Explain how the flashbacks about Gina's family enhance our understanding of the present situation.

3. What would have happened to Gina's family if she hadn't made sacrifices for it?

4. Discuss the tensions between Gina's role as a godmother to Marisol and her role as a sister to Ugo.

5. To what extent does Gina achieve a balance between her responsibilities for her family and her desire for self-fulfillment?

6. How did Marisol's adoptive parents complicate her sense of identity?

7. Comment on the use of drugs to make Marisol conform to the image of her adoptive parents. To what extent is the use of drugs for this purpose a societal issue?

8. Why was Marisol attracted to the virtual world of the internet? Was it beneficial for her?

9. How do the meetings between Gina and Colman and the therapist and the psychiatrist enhance your understanding of Marisol's disorder?

10. What do Gina and Colman believe is the most effective treatment for this disorder?

11. What did Marisol reveal about herself in the persona she created on Facebook?

12. If you were Gina's friend, why would you have introduced her to Colman?

13. How does Colman's mission help in the search for Marisol?

14. Explain why Marisol needs to find her birth mother.

15. How does it affect Marisol when she discovers what really happened to her birth mother?

16. What do you think Marisol will do when they get home?